Toasted

TOASTED
A BROOM CLOSET MYSTERY

MARIANNA ROBERG

Toasted

To my parents. Thanks for believing in me.

Toasted

Acknowledgments

I'm going to miss thanking people. I'm sorry.

Many, many thanks to Sergeant Damian Hogan, of An Garda Síochána Press and Public Relations Office, for answering my questions about police procedure in Ireland. He even offered to call all the way from Dublin to answer my questions. And on a holiday, too! Any mistakes herein are entirely my own.

I also could not have done this book without the help of Kathryn Olsen, who said one night on Facebook, "Tickets to Ireland are $360 right now, but I don't have anyone to go with!" Thanks for suggesting it, and for going with me and spending a week doing random things like wandering down alleys in Dublin and having lunch in the Christ Church Cathedral crypt!

Also, thanks to everyone who read "Pasted" and liked it. I appreciate that.

Toasted

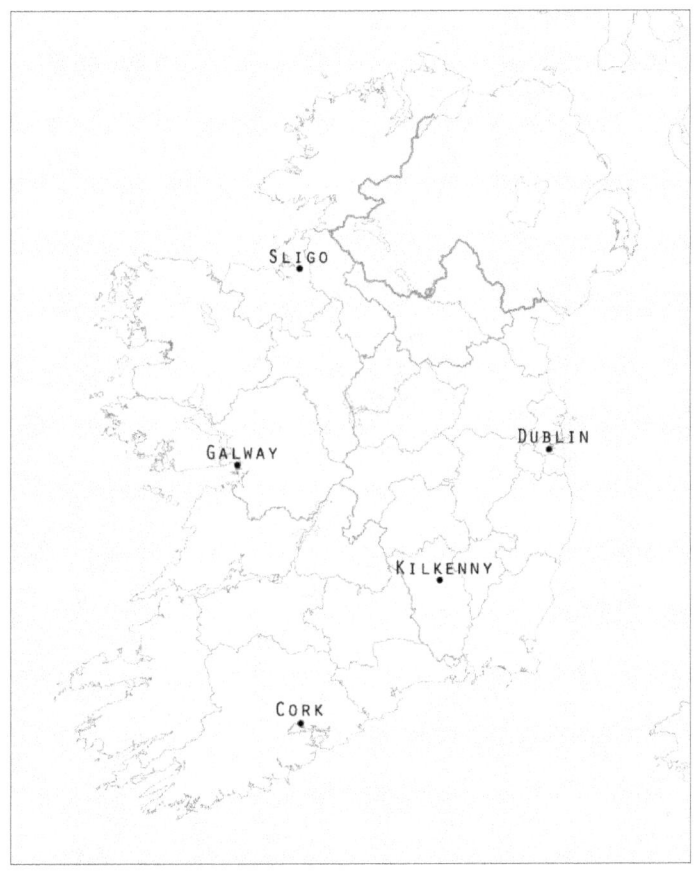

Toasted

CHAPTER ONE

It was a bright sunny morning. The birds were singing; warm rays of sunlight shone through my bedroom window. It would have been wonderful, if my cat hadn't been sitting in my ivory-painted windowsill, making "ik-ik-ik" noises at the robin nesting in the tree just outside.

I groaned and heaved one of the pillows towards the offending animal, my beloved four-footed roommate Angelus. The pillow missed, but the cat shut up and jumped off the sill to join me on the bed. For several minutes, I half-heartedly fended off furry affection.

After a while of trying to stick his tongue up

my nose, Angelus abandoned me and went back to the sill, mercifully quiet this time as he eyed the winged snacks just beyond his grasp. I sat up to find a ghost perched on the end of my bed.

"Mom! A little warning!" I gasped out.

"You should be used to this by now," my mother said tartly. "By the way, there's a naked man in the back yard."

I blinked at her for a long moment, then tossed back the covers and bolted out of bed. My room was at the front of the house, so I had to dash downstairs and out to the back porch before I could really get a good look.

To my disappointment, the man in my back yard wasn't naked. He *was* shirtless, however, and that improved my morning considerably. He also had a broadsword, and was swinging it in a series of complicated exercises.

Not much caring that I was still in my sleepwear—yoga pants and a tank top with a built-in bra—I fetched a glass of the strawberry lemonade I'd fixed the night before and stepped outside to admire the Celtic warrior who'd invaded my property.

His name was Milo Hennessy, and he was six-feet, four-and-a-half inches of Irish muscle, a good deal of which was on display in the late April morning light. He'd left his shirt draped over the railing, near where I stood, so he was clad only in old jeans and a battered pair of boots he'd brought with him from Ireland the autumn before.

Mom came through the wall beside me and we both admired my boyfriend. I didn't mind her doing it, really; she was dead. And he *was* very nice to look at. He had two tattoos, one that encircled his right bicep, and one of a stag on his right shoulder blade. He would have looked at home on just about any romance novel cover. Even after six months, I couldn't believe he'd picked me.

After a few moments, Mom wandered back into the house, leaving me alone with my boyfriend.

"Nice sword," I called.

Milo jumped and lost his grip on the weapon, which sank at least three inches into the grass at his feet, narrowly missing his toes. Oops. His expletive was breathless and unrepeatable. Green eyes narrowed at me, he paused to push shoulder-length black curls out of his face. I had to forcibly remind myself to breathe.

I wanted to hop the railing and climb him like a tree. What I did was take a demure sip of lemonade, then offer him the glass. He approached and accepted the glass held over the railing.

"Any particular reason you're swinging that thing in my back yard?" I asked.

"My apartment's too small," he said, once he'd swallowed. He was right, his apartment was way too small for what he'd been doing. He could barely stand up straight in his living room. "An' I knew ya wouldn't mind."

I grinned, leaning over the rail to kiss him. The fact that the porch was three feet up from ground level actually made kissing him easier; he was a handful of inches more than a foot taller than me, and I barely reached his shoulder in three-inch-heels.

"Mornin' t'ya, *cailín*," he murmured against my lips.

Then he dragged me over the railing. I shrieked as my feet left the ground, but a second later I was pinned against him, and had no more air to scream with. He laughed and kissed me again, before setting me down.

I took a moment to recover, because being pressed against his bare chest had scrambled my brain. I cleared my throat, shook my head, and focused instead on the sword he'd brought over.

"I haven't seen this one before," I commented. The massive weapon was nearly as tall as me, but done in the Celtic style, with the leaf-shaped blade and the man-shaped handle and pommel. "Is it new?"

Milo yanked the blade out of the ground and tipped it in the sunlight, letting the rays flash off the polished steel surface. The handle was a brilliant gold, wrapped in leather and gold wire, and the blade bore inscriptions in very old Gaelic lettering in the blood groove.

"It's an early birthday gift," he told me in a low voice. "From my da."

My mental gears ground to a halt, as they usually did when the subject of his paternal family came up. "Wait. I thought that you'd never met your father."

"I haven't. Found it in a really long wooden box in me livin' room this mornin'." His accent had thickened, as it tended to in emotional moments. "With a note, tellin' me it was from my dear ol' dad, wishin' me a happy birthday an' sayin' he hoped t'see me soon."

I gulped. Milo's father was something of a shadowy figure to us, a man Milo had never met and I sort of hoped never to; for starters, his name was Lugh and at one point, he'd been worshipped as a god of war.

Milo shoved the blade back into the ground and studied it for a long moment. Curiosity had me trying to lift it. I couldn't budge the thing.

"Dang, that's heavy."

"That's 'cause it's real," he said shortly.

I raised both eyebrows and reached for it again. This time, I opened the shielding I'd been practicing to keep around myself, to prevent unwanted clairvoyant visions at awkward moments.

The last time Milo had received something from his father, an ancient gold torque, it had given me a vision so powerful that it had literally knocked me flat. The scars from where it burned me still crossed my palms. I prepared myself as best I could, just in case I was in for a repeat.

The buzzing started just before I touched it. Very cautiously, I closed my hand around the handle. It was like an electric current ran over the surface of the sword, but I didn't pick up any visuals. Milo was right, though, the sword was authentic, and incredibly old.

I shook my hands when I let go. It wasn't an unpleasant feeling, but it wasn't one I wanted to repeat anytime soon. Touching it was out, but it sure was pretty to look at. Sadly, that largely extended to my relationship with Milo.

"What does that say?" I asked, gesturing to the engraved wording.

My boyfriend picked up the sword, seemingly without effort, and studied the blade. "*'Sa Fhírinne'*," he said, sounding somewhat doubtful. "It's in Old Irish, so I'm mostly guessin'. If that's what it says, it means somethin' like 'in truth' or . . . *'sa'* could also mean 'sword' or 'knife', so it might be 'truth sword'."

"That's kinda cheesy."

"It's a sword, *cailín*. It isn't gonna have poetry on it."

"Good point. Um. Is there any reason Lugh decided that you needed a sword for your birthday? Are ties or trust funds just not done in Faerie?"

Milo snorted. He pulled a hair elastic out of one pocket and tied his hair back, off his face. I tried not to drool on his chest.

"I dunno," he admitted. "Since I haven't spoken t'him."

"Hmm. You think he'll make an appearance at Muriel's wedding?"

He shrugged. "Guess we'll find out when we get there."

***

Packing is not one of my strong suits. I always put it off to the last minute, even when I've got weeks to prepare. Two days after Milo's shirtless visit, I was up in my room, agonizing over what to bring with me to Ireland.

Mom sat on my bed, in the middle of a pile of

discarded shirts, and said, "Relax, honey, you're not dressing for paparazzi."

"Thanks, Mom. I just . . . don't want to look like a hobo when I meet Milo's mom."

"Then you definitely don't want to wear that," she said of the shirt in my hand.

I held up the sweater. "What's wrong with this? It's warm, and Milo says the weather might be cool there."

"It has a hole in the shoulder you never remember to fix."

"Oh, right." I added the sweater to the pile, then flopped down across the full-size bed and stared at the ceiling. "I'm going to Ireland tomorrow."

"Which is why you should be packing, not lounging around."

"Says the ghost."

My room was painted a soothing, sage green, the wainscotting and trim all a creamy ivory. The only exception was the fireplace, made of hand-carved oak. I also had a black, wrought-iron spiral staircase off to one side, leading up to a "loft" in the circular tower. A poster of Jack Sparrow from *Pirates Of The Caribbean* occupied the back of the bathroom door.

"Have Maegan come over and help you pack," Mom suggested.

I rolled to my side and looked at her. "That's a good idea. Thanks."

A ball of black fur came flying onto the bed. Angelus landed with an "urf!" and immediately burrowed into the pile of shirts. I moved to extricate him and got chewed for my efforts.

"Crazy cat," I muttered.

Deciding to leave the fuzzy lunatic where he was, I went to call Maegan.

***

"You nervous about meeting Milo's family?"

I paused in loading my last suitcase into the back of Milo's truck cab. My best friend, Maegan Willard, had come over to see us off. Mags had her long, red hair braided, dressed in jeans and a purple tank top that clashed with her hair. But that was Mags; somehow, she made it work.

"A little," I admitted. "But if this relationship continues, which I hope it will, I'll probably do it sooner or later."

Milo came out of the house with my cat in a carrier. As soon as I'd fetched the carrier out of the attic, Angelus had done a disappearing act; my boyfriend had located him atop the cupboards in the kitchen, and had spent the last fifteen minutes getting the furball down, since I was way too short to reach.

"Hi, kitty!" Maegan cooed at the yowling cat. She took the carrier from Milo. "You're lucky that I moved back in with Rhoda and Archie. My old landlord wouldn't have let me take Angelus."

"Oh, believe me. I know how lucky I am, and how unfortunate you are." I grinned.

"Actually, Uncle Archie isn't that bad. He pretty much stays in the den these days, and I only see him at meals."

Maegan had lived in an apartment located in a converted 1920s craftsman across town, but her uncle's failing health had prompted her to move in with her aunt, the owner of the store where we all worked. Archie was fat, and while Rhoda wasn't skinny, there was no way she could help her husband by herself if something should happen. I understood it; I just didn't like it, because Archie was, well . . . Archie. The Guffmans, and now Mags once again, lived a few blocks west of me. Maegan had been raised by them after the death of her mother.

Mags wandered over to her rusty--I mean, *trusty*--robin's egg blue VW Beetle and put the carrier in the passenger seat. Milo leaned past me to rearrange one of the suitcases, then shut the back door of the truck.

"So, our flight leaves insanely early," I told her. "We're gonna spend the night with Milo's cousin in Salt Lake, then fly out. The wedding's on the fourth, we're staying in Dublin through the twelfth, when we fly back. Our flight back won't land until really late, so I should be by on the thirteenth to fetch the cat."

"Got it." She nodded. "Have fun, bring me Doctor Who stuff."

"That's a British show," I pointed out.

"Yeah, but there's a comics store right on the River Liffey, at the edge of Temple Bar. I looked it up. Bring me back cool stuff." Mags gave me a tight hug, and whispered, "And try to get laid, will ya?"

My face flaming, I pulled away and pretended to sock her in the shoulder. She laughed and skipped out of reach.

"What?" Milo asked.

"Nothing," we replied in unison.

I glanced at my watch. "Okay, we gotta go. See you in a couple weeks!"

CHAPTER TWO

I hadn't flown anywhere in several years. In fact, I hadn't been out of the country since I was twelve and Mom took me to England on a tour of castles. It had been for a book about haunted ones, and we'd left after I'd seen one too many spirits, mainly a young woman named Anne Boleyn who liked to carry her head under her arm.

But she'd insisted I keep my passport up to date, so I hadn't had to worry about the expense after she'd died and my household income dropped drastically. I couldn't really afford this trip, but when I'd been invited, I couldn't say no. I loved Milo, and this was a big deal to him.

That said, I was thrilled to board our plane to

Atlanta, where we'd connect to a flight to Dublin. I wasn't looking forward to spending that long cramped in coach, but Milo had the raw deal, having to cram his long legs into the narrow row.

We'd left Mike Flaherty's place in Salt Lake City at a little past four in the morning, finally boarding a half hour before our seven o'clock flight. We spent almost eight hours in Atlanta, a larger part of it spent wandering around the various terminals, since they wouldn't give us our boarding passes for the second leg of the journey--or even tell us what gate we were at--until two hours before the flight.

Atlanta is the largest airport I've ever been in, that I can recall, and it was crowded. I'm not really a people-person, so I stuck close to Milo as we dragged our carry-ons around with us. We ate lunch at Chili's, then hit the duty-free shop in the international terminal.

I made Milo help me pick out a lipstick at the MAC mini-store. He rolled his eyes a few times, but was a good sport about it, over all. I ended up getting an insanely-red lipstick that I wouldn't normally have chosen, but it *did* match the red slinky top Mags had made me pack. I wasn't sure when or if I was going to wear it, but I had it in case I needed it.

Once we'd taken off, I had to laugh as Milo struggled to make himself comfortable, his legs folded tightly under the tray table he'd put his laptop on. The row we were in was miniscule, and when the man in the seat in front leaned it back, things only got worse. Milo narrowed his eyes at me and I tried but failed to appear contrite.

"What are ya laughin' at?" he asked.

"I'm imagining you trying to join the mile high club in that teeny, tiny bathroom and getting stuck."

Then I realized what I'd said and turned brilliant red as he slowly lifted one corner of his sensual mouth.

"An' with whom were ya imagining me doin' this?" he asked.

"Um." I cleared my throat. "Oh, look, the drink cart!"

I was grateful for the distraction and accepted a Diet Coke. I don't sleep well in front of strangers and wanted to stay awake as long as possible. I'd probably crash once we reached our destination, but until then, I was going to be wired.

Milo didn't press the question he'd posed and I retreated into a Terry Goodkind novel while he worked on the speech he'd give as the best man.

As the flight attendants began passing out dinner, I realized that one of them was a little different. Her hair wasn't quite up to date, and her uniform wasn't the same as the others. It was when one of the attendants pushed the drink cart *through* her that it clicked.

I nudged Milo. He grunted. I nudged harder and he finally looked up.

"What?"

"Woman at two o'clock," I murmured. "The blonde with the big bangs."

He looked over, then wrinkled his nose and turned back to me. "Oh. You gonna . . . ?"

"Not if I can help it," I told him. "I want this trip to be ghost free."

Famous last words, naturally.

***

I fell asleep somewhere over the Atlantic, which was a completely unimpressive black nothingness outside the window of the plane when I drifted off in the middle of a Ben Stiller movie. Somehow, the crew was chipper when they woke us for breakfast. I'd dozed off with my head against Milo's shoulder. He didn't say a word about the drool on his sleeve, and I went along with it.

My first glimpse of Ireland was a brilliant green blur through misty clouds. Then the clouds parted, and the landscape was stunning beyond words, as we flew over the Cliffs of Moher. The vivid green of the land was almost painful after the brown grass of Utah. Out the window, I saw green fields in crazy shapes, the ruins of ancient ring forts, and little cottages scattered between bustling little towns.

On the ground in Dublin, we gathered our luggage. I already felt out of place with the accents of everyone rolling around me like waves. The man who stamped my passport was a delightful older gent, who wished me a very warm welcome to Ireland.

Then we stepped outside.

"I can't believe I'm here," I said. "I've wanted to come here since I was thirteen."

"Wait'll we actually get to real soil," he murmured. "I'm tellin' you now, brace yerself."

I looped my arm through his. "Really?"

"Oh, yeah. It's like nothin' else I've ever felt." He paused. "'Cept when I'm kissin' you."

I tripped at his words and he spun me into his arms, dropping his backpack to do so. Milo lifted me in his arms to kiss me. Someone nearby whistled and I laughed.

"C'mon," he said. "Let's go meet Muriel."

As we walked out to get the rental car, I was glad I'd taken his advice. When I stepped onto a grass divider, my knees nearly buckled from the rush of . . . something . . . that swelled up through me. Only his arm linked with mine kept me upright.

"What . . ." I sucked in a huge breath and tried again. "What was that?"

"I'm not sure, exactly," he said as he hauled me towards the rental cars. "Power? What's left from thousands o' years of magic races livin' here? You'll get usedta it."

I wasn't so sure. It was a steady buzz around me as we got in the car. I could only imagine what it was going to be like once we got out of the city and into the countryside, where the wedding would be held.

Milo explained as we drove that his mother had gone, briefly, to Trinity College before she'd had to drop out when he and his sister had been born. He and Muriel had opted to attend UCD Dublin because the program Muriel wanted hadn't been offered at Trinity and where his twin went, so did Milo. Muriel's fiancé had been Milo's dorm-mate; Milo had introduced them and soon they'd been inseparable. I thought it was very sweet.

Muriel and her fiancé, Quinn, lived north of the river Liffey, on the outskirts in a community called Hollystown, but owned a jewelry shop on the edge of Temple Bar in south Dublin. Milo drove as if he'd never left, navigating the narrow, winding streets with a surety I would have never managed. Pedestrians ran out in front of the car, prompting him to slam on the brakes multiple times. I would have been screaming obscenities at the suicidal residents, but he took it in stride.

He parked in a pay lot and we walked two blocks that were densely packed with tall, narrow buildings, most of them dark brick or pale grey granite. I snapped a bunch of pictures, in awe of it all. Milo stood and waited patiently by a recessed entryway, under a gaily-painted sign that read "*Leathlómhara - Seodra*", and under that, "Jewellery by Muriel". The shop door was apple green, and had a bell that jangled when Milo pushed it open to duck inside. I took a moment to admire the pale woodwork and light pastel walls. Every available surface had been used to display a fascinating array of jewels and baubles. While it was obvious that the building, and thus the shop, was old, the windows were large enough to admit plenty of light. A good deal of my nervousness at meeting Milo's literal other half bled away in the relaxing and cheerful environment.

A young couple was in the shop with their daughter, who looked to be all of four. The father had the girl up in his arms so she could inspect some necklaces hung cleverly on the chandelier. I exchanged a brief smile with the mother and trailed after Milo as he headed towards the back, where his sister and her fiancé waited.

There was an exclamation in Gaeilge, and then

a tall, dark-haired whirlwind attacked Milo. I cleared out of the way and found myself standing next to a fairly non-descript young man with prematurely balding brown hair, glasses, and a genial smile.

"Best to let them at it, yeah?" he offered, then held out his hand. "I'm Quinn. O'Donnell. Muriel's fiancé."

"Peyton Reynolds," I said. "Milo's girlfriend."

The twins were still conversing rapidly in Gaelic. I didn't catch a word of it.

"I don't understand, either," Quinn confided, reading the lack of comprehension on my face.

Milo chose that moment to reach one long arm out and snag me to drag me over to meet his sister.

On first meeting Muriel Hennessy, it would have been insanely easy to hate her. She was, to the human eye, perfect. Just shy of six feet tall, she was lithe and somehow delicately boned. She was graced with big green eyes under a cascade of waist-length black curls, full lips, and a feminine version of Milo's aquiline nose.

She was also incredibly sweet and effervescent, and smiled broadly when she saw me. "You must be Peyton!" she burbled. "Milo's told me all about ya."

I glanced at my boyfriend, who just grinned at me.

"An' I see you're wearin' the necklace I made," she continued.

I turned my gaze to the pendant that hung just above my cleavage, a matrix opal from Australia, black with brilliant green and blue flecks radiating in the sterling silver setting. Milo had given it to me for

Christmas, after visiting his family over the holiday. "Yeah," I told her. "I just about never take it off."

She smiled; I knew I'd won brownie points with her by wearing it. I wanted Milo's family to like me, and it seemed I was off to a great start.

CHAPTER THREE

Muriel closed up shop and we followed her to the northern outskirts of Dublin. She and Quinn had a cute little free-standing house with a fairly sizable yard. Half red brick, half tan stucco, it was something of a mishmash of construction, but from what I'd seen so far, it fit Muriel to a T.

"So what does Quinn do?" I asked Milo as he parked the car.

"He runs the day t' day stuff for Muriel, while she makes the jewelry. She's brilliant w' metal, but doesn't have a head fer numbers at all."

"Kinda like Maegan," I remarked.

He hauled our bags out of the car and up to the door. Muriel met him there and chattered nonstop in

Irish, while Quinn and I followed more sedately.

"I hear you met Milo through work," he said to me as we went up the walk.

I nodded. "We work together at a store called The Broom Closet."

He cocked his head. "What's the reason for that title?"

I had to smile. "Being 'in the broom closet' is being a secretly-practicing Wiccan or Pagan. You're not 'out'."

Quinn laughed. "That's clever."

"I'm not responsible," I said. "That would be my boss, Rhoda. Her husband, Archie, hired Milo on a whim. Best thing he's ever done."

We entered the house. Muriel met us at the door. "You're in the bedroom upstairs, front of the house and to the right. I thought you'd appreciate the ensuite."

"Oh, thanks. Yes." I was pleased that she hadn't assumed Milo and I were sleeping together.

Upstairs, I saw Milo had put my bags next to the bed I'd be using. He was down the short hallway, in a room that overlooked the back garden. I knocked on the open door.

"Have you told Muriel about your dad yet?" I asked him.

He grimaced. "No."

"She's getting married in three days. You might want to do that. I'm sure Quinn will want to know his fiancée is part-Sidhe and part-Fomori."

He sighed. "Right. I better do that now, huh?"

"I'd want to know."

Milo turned and trudged down the stairs. I

followed at a distance, to let Milo sequester Muriel in her home office, just off the entrance hall. I joined her fiancé in the kitchen. Quinn raised an eyebrow at me.

"They have some sibling stuff to discuss," I began.

Then Muriel started shouting. It was in their native tongue, so I couldn't make out a word of it, but it sounded colorful. The longer it went on, the higher Quinn's brows went.

"So. You've known Milo a while, huh?"

"Mmm. Shared a dorm our freshman year. Played rugby at UCD together, too."

"I didn't know Milo played rugby," I said with some surprise.

Quinn gave me a half-smile. "Big guy like that? All the recruiters wanted 'im. But he didn't wanna do it, after a while."

I pondered that. If Milo had gone pro, would we have ever met? Not something I wanted to consider too much, considering how I felt about him.

Eventually, the twins emerged from the office. Muriel was red-faced and sullen; Milo looked frustrated and tired. Quinn suggested that we all pile into the car and drive out to show us around the church where they were getting married in a few days.

That seemed to brighten Muriel up. She still didn't look at Milo, her anger evident in her rigid spine.

"Went better'n I expected," my boyfriend murmured as we got in the car. "She didn't try t'kill me."

Since the happy couple lived in Dublin, and Quinn's parents didn't live *too* far to the south, Muriel and her fiancé were getting married at his parents' parish church in Glencullen. It was located fairly out of the way, about an hour outside the city. That, of course, was only due to tiny roads and an abnormally low speed limit, at least by my standards. Even the motorway's limit was on par with our largest surface streets back home, a measly forty miles an hour.

I wasn't familiar with Catholic churches, but I instantly loved this one, with its old, weathered stone and the cemetery behind it. Ordinarily, I hated cemeteries, but this one was full of fascinating headstones. I'd have to steal a bit of time and go investigate; I didn't see any wandering spirits as we got out of the car.

Milo had been right; while the buzz of power was obviously stronger out here, it no longer made me dizzy. That was something I greatly appreciated, because I already loved Ireland and didn't want to be metaphysically allergic to the place.

Muriel's cell phone rang and she answered it as Milo and I looked around the churchyard. "*Dia duit,* Mam*! Conas atá tú? Gleann Cuilinn teampall.*"

While she was talking, I wandered over to the cemetery. It was actually a peaceful one, rather old, though some of the graves were newer. I saw a flicker that might have been a ghost, but it didn't stay long enough for me to tell. Most graveyards are rife with spirit activity, but this one seemed to have restful residents.

Milo tagged along, lost in his own thoughts, as

I weaved through the Celtic crosses and the angels. Muriel shouted to us when she was done with her call, and informed us that their mother was on her way and would join us in about half an hour.

We stepped inside the church. It was an adorable little chapel, with a high, pointed arch ceiling and a window display at the front. It was stained glass now, but probably hadn't been originally. Exposed beams supported the roof, dark against the whitewashed walls. Pews lined both sides of the single aisle.

Smaller windows gave a view of the green landscape to the left, the rectory visible through the windows to the right. I made my way up the aisle to have a better look at the windows.

"We're gonna have an aisle runner, o' course, and Mam's found someone real lovely for doin' the flowers, they'll be at the ends of the benches here." Muriel sounded so happy and enthusiastic, it was impossible not to be infected by it. I found myself smiling as she gushed to her big brother about her plans. At least she wasn't upset by Milo's news anymore. If she was, she was hiding it really well.

Milo smiled indulgently and stepped up to join me by the altar. "This church was built around the time of the Famine," he told me. "It's got a lot o' history to it."

Movement out of the corner of my eye caught my attention, and I glanced towards the doors through which we'd entered. A young woman stood in the aisle, staring at us. Her hair was long and brown; I couldn't tell what color her eyes were, but they were focused intently on us. There was something unsettling about how she stared.

I opened my mouth to speak to her, but before I could get any words out, Muriel walked right through her.

"Yeah," I said, with just a touch of irony. "I can tell."

Milo followed my gaze. "Ah," he murmured.

Abruptly, the girl vanished. Muriel was completely oblivious, still chattering about the decorations and the ceremony. I glanced at Milo with a raised eyebrow.

"Can she . . .?" I whispered.

"Not like we can," he answered. "Her abilities are . . . different. Most of 'em came out as creative stuff. Which *does* come from Da."

"Ah."

A horn beeped outside, and a few moments later, a harried-looking older woman bustled in. She wore jeans and a wool cardigan, her black curls gathered in a haphazard knot at the back of her head. Her eyes were blue, with little crows' feet around them. But she was beautiful still, perhaps in her early forties, and I could tell instantly where the twins got their looks.

"Mam!" Milo exclaimed. He rushed forward and enveloped the woman in a bear-hug, lifting her clear off her feet.

Eithne Hennessy laughed and said, "Put me down, you lug."

I watched the family reunion with a smile, keeping an eye out for the ghost. It was habit, one not easily broken.

Milo pulled his mother over to where I stood.

"Mam, this is Peyton. Peyton, I'd like ya t'meet my mother, Eithne Hennessy."

"It's really nice to meet you," I told her.

She ignored my offered hand, which had been a big gesture on my part since I tried not to touch people, and hugged me. "*Dia duit*, Peyton. It's so wonderful t' finally meet the girl me Milo raves about."

When she let me go, I raised a brow at Milo, who smiled somewhat enigmatically. I was seriously going to have to find out what he'd been telling people that made them want to hug me.

It was decided that we'd go to dinner back in Dublin, to celebrate the twins' birthday, which happened to be that day. I didn't think that if I ever got married, I'd do it near my birthday, because if things went south, I wouldn't want the two connected.

Truthfully, though, I didn't see Muriel and Quinn having problems. All I got from either of them was a sense of years of bliss, which was pleasing.

Since it was Milo's birthday--and Muriel's, obviously--I'd brought his present with me to Ireland and tucked it in my purse. I'd also brought something for Muriel, though I wasn't really sure what kinds of things she liked.

Over dessert, I gave them their presents. Muriel exclaimed that I shouldn't have, but really, what kind of jerk wouldn't? She tore the wrapping paper off and made "ooh" and "ahh" noises over the present: it was a sterling silver cuff bracelet, with a turquoise cabochon and Navajo tribal designs on it.

"I figured you probably haven't seen much Native American stuff," I said. "So I thought I'd bring you something from where I'm from."

"Oh, it's lovely! Thanks so much!" She got up, came around the table, and hugged me again.

At least she wasn't giving off anything to read, save for the faint smell of the ocean I always got in the back of my head when Milo was around. It had gotten to the point where I barely noticed, except when Milo was feeling homesick.

"Now what'd you get my brother?" she demanded as she settled back in her seat.

Eithne rolled her eyes at her daughter. "Let him open his present, *a iníon*, for heaven's sake."

"She's been like this since we were little," Milo told me, loud enough for his sister to hear. "When we were kids, she'd steal me presents an' open 'em herself."

"What can I say?" Muriel responded. "I like shiny things."

We all laughed. Milo turned his attention to the present I'd given him. He unwrapped a stainless steel card case, with an etched plaid design and the monogram "MCMH".

"Ahh," he said, and smiled. "I been lookin' for one o' these things."

"I know. So I got one for you. Happy birthday, babe." I leaned over and kissed his cheek. "I have something else, too, but you'll get it later."

He looked very interested at that. Sadly, if he thought it involved me in lingerie, he was going to be disappointed.

CHAPTER FOUR

I hadn't anticipated so much activity after our flight, and I was exhausted. I fell asleep in the car on the way back, only rousing when Milo gently shook my shoulder.

I collapsed into bed and didn't wake 'til after dawn. The others were already up. Muriel was making jewelry at the kitchen table, while Quinn cooked breakfast alongside Eithne. Milo was reading the morning paper.

"Good, you're up!" Muriel said on seeing me. I noticed that her accent was a little less pronounced than Milo's, probably from being in Dublin and around its international residents so much longer.

I frowned and dragged my hair back into a ponytail. "Did you need me for something?"

Muriel glanced at her brother, then smiled at me. "Well, I know we just met yesterday, but I was wonderin' if you'd be one of my bridesmaids, for the wedding."

I blinked. "Really?"

Quinn, at the stove, said, "Milo's my best man. Wouldn't be fair to leave his girl out."

Muriel nodded. Milo was watching me over the top of the newspaper. "See," his sister said, "I've got a Maid o' Honor, but I could use another bridesmaid, sure."

I was flattered, and didn't see any reason to refuse. "Okay."

"Yay!" the bride piped. I had to laugh at her enthusiasm. "We'll go shoppin' today."

***

"I have to wear a hat?" I asked, looking between Muriel and her mother. "No one said anything about a hat."

"Don't worry," Eithne said. "I'm sure Muriel knows all the best places to get hats in the city."

"I do," the bride said. "An' we'll get ya into a pretty dress, too. I mean, I'm sure what ya brought's lovely, but it probably won't match me colors. Let's leave the boys t' their plottin' an' go shopping!"

Thus, I found myself dragged out into the bustling streets. Muriel thought that I'd look best in either fuchsia or turquoise. I vetoed the pink and we compromised on either apple green or the blue. I swore that when I got married, I'd only have two colors, and they'd be easy to find.

After three hours going through various stores, I found a gorgeous gown at a store by St. Stephen's Green: a floor-length, turquoise satin number with a black lace overlay and three little black straps at each shoulder. Black beaded lace decorated the sweetheart neckline. As expected, the difficult part was the hat. I don't usually wear hats, as they aren't part of normal day wear--or *any* wear, really--back in the US. And the hats at the place we visited were all covered in feathers and things.

"My cat will kill this," I said of the headpiece I eventually picked out. It was expensive, over a hundred and fifty euro, money I didn't really have to spend. But I wanted to do what I could, and it was really pretty: turquoise straw with black, blue, and turquoise feathers, lace, and beading.

Muriel snatched the hat out of my hand. "My gift t'you," she said before I could protest. "You're doin' me a humongous favor, an' you've no idea how long I've waited t'see my stupid brother look at a girl the way he looks at you."

"I couldn't possibly-" I began, and she snorted.

"Oh, do shut up," she said sweetly. "Milo was right, you're a stubborn wee thing."

I didn't know whether to take offense or thank her.

***

After dinner that night, Muriel announced that I needed to meet "the girls". I gave Milo a helpless look, but he just waved jauntily as his twin dragged me out to her "hen night". He thought it was hilarious that I was letting Muriel haul me around.

We met at a trendy little café on the edge of Temple Bar. Muriel's best friend, a girl named Darcy Ahearn, was her Maid of Honor. Darcy was tall and kind of angular, with light blonde hair and big, brown doe eyes. She handed out strings of pink Mardi Gras type beads, with little fuchsia shot glasses attached to them, and plopped a hat on Muriel's head that declared "Bachelorette".

"Sorry," she said to me. "I didn't know ya were comin', so there isn't anythin' for ya."

"That's okay," I said, waving it off. "I don't drink, anyway. I'm just along for the ride."

Muriel hugged my arm. "This is Peyton, from America. She's my brother's girl, and she'll be my sister soon, if I've a say in it!"

I blushed a little, surprised at her words. Something flickered on Darcy's face, but she quickly disguised it and gestured to the other girls in our party.

"Well. Isn't that somethin'. This is Ciara Murphy," Darcy said. Ciara had sleek, dark brown hair and kind of looked like she was already sloshed.

Then I was introduced to Nell Robinson, a very strikingly pretty black woman with shoulder-length curls, and her roommate Rose Collins, who was on the mousier side, like me, with dishwater hair and bright blue eyes.

"Hi, nice to meet you," Nell said, shaking my hand. She was English, so I didn't feel quite as outnumbered by the Irish. "America, huh? What part?"

"Utah," I supplied.

"Oh, yeah. I had a modeling gig out there a few years back, when I was working in Los Angeles. We did a shoot at, what's it called, Zion?" Nell smiled. "Beautiful area."

"Zion's is a few hours south of where I live," I told her. I shook hands with Rose and Ciara, as well.

"Sooo, you're goin' with Milo, yeah?" Ciara asked. She glanced at Darcy, then nudged Nell.

I was definitely getting a vibe now. Something was up with Darcy and Milo. Exes? He'd told me he hadn't left anyone behind when he'd come to America, so if there had been anything between them, it was long enough ago that Milo hadn't thought it worth mentioning.

The party was a pub crawl. I tagged along awkwardly, wishing I hadn't let Muriel coerce me so easily. At the fourth bar, the bride asked why I wasn't drinking.

"I don't," I told her. "I never have."

She arched a brow at me. "Not at all? You must think we're the biggest lushes."

I smiled and shook my head. "It's fine. You need a designated sheep herder, anyway."

Muriel let out a cackle at that, throwing her head back. "Oh, you're funny! I like you. Much better for Milo than Darcy."

I glanced around. Darcy wasn't present, having taken herself off to the restroom. Muriel seemed to realize what she'd said about her Maid of Honor and clapped a hand over her mouth.

"Terrible thing o' me t'say," she said then. "I

didn't even think. You've figured out Milo usedta go wi' Darcy, haven't ya? It was quite a few years ago, so it didn't occur to me. Sorry."

"My ex lives with me," I said. "But he's dead."

Her brows drew together, reminded of what her brother had told her the day before. "Oh, he's a ghost? Gad. Thrown me for a loop, Milo has. Dunno how I'm gonna tell Quinn 'bout this."

"You're getting married in two days, you might want to figure it out."

She sighed and nodded. "Yeah."

Personally, I'd expected Milo to tell her back at Christmas, but he hadn't. From what I'd seen of Quinn so far, I didn't think he'd do anything drastic when she told him. He was pretty laid back. And he'd known the twins far longer than I had. I'd figured out what Milo was within a week of knowing him, so chances were pretty good Quinn suspected. That is, if he believed in that sort of thing.

We hit one more pub, then the party scattered to the winds. The rehearsal was the next evening, and the wedding the morning after. I was the only one who wasn't going to be nursing a hangover in the morning. I wouldn't be surprised if I somehow ended up being the one to round everyone up for the festivities tomorrow.

I also got to drive Muriel home, which was an adventure in itself. I managed not to crash, and I only freaked out about the traffic circles once. All in all, a pretty successful evening.

***

Milo was waiting when we got back. He helped his sister get up the stairs, then joined me in the kitchen.

"Headache?" he asked, watching as I downed a pain reliever.

"Start of one. I'm not used to being around that many people for that long, and my shielding isn't quite up to it," I admitted.

He came over and began rubbing my neck, his long fingers kneading the tight muscles. "Thanks for helpin' Muriel. I know it's put ya in a strange position, but I appreciate it a lot."

I failed at containing a groan and leaned into his hands. "I've never been a bridesmaid before, actually. It was fun talking with everyone . . . when they weren't drinking."

He pushed my hair over my shoulders and leaned down to kiss the nape of my neck. I shivered and turned my head. Milo kissed the side of my throat, then my jaw. I turned in his arms; he pulled me close and lifted me off my feet to set me on the counter.

"How was the stag night?" I asked.

"Eh. Fine. We played darts, had a few drinks. There were no strippers."

I laughed and ran my fingers through his hair. "Ciara and Nell did a table dance."

Milo pressed his lips to the palm of my hand. "An' what'd you do?"

"Missed you."

I kissed him, trying to pour into it everything that I felt. His arms went tight around me and he returned the kiss hungrily, possessively. He'd never

Toasted

quite kissed me that way before.

"We could go upstairs," he whispered against my mouth.

"Your mom's asleep up there," I pointed out.

Milo sighed and pulled away, just a bit but enough to give us both air. "Right. Ah, well."

He ran his fingers gently down the side of my face. "Go get some sleep, *cailín*."

Reluctantly, I hopped off the counter and left him at the kitchen door. I trudged up the stairs and retreated to my borrowed bedroom.

I was out as soon as my head hit my pillow, but it was not a deep or dreamless sleep. Fire chased me through empty hallways and stone caverns. A glimpse of black eyes in a pale, laughing face woke me in a cold sweat.

I'd seen that face before, but where?

CHAPTER FIVE

We arrived at the rehearsal a little after five in the evening on Saturday. I noted that Ciara wasn't present. It was Rose who informed me that Ciara had work and wouldn't be along until the wedding in the morning.

"Oh. Is that why Muriel conned me into being an extra?" I asked.

Rose laughed. "That an' she's got a complete thing for you an' Milo. She's been goin' on about meetin' you since Milo told her about you at Christmas."

"I see." I looked around the chapel. "So, about Darcy . . ."

"Don't worry about her," Rose assured me.

"They grew up together, so it was sort of assumed, I hear, that they'd end up married or whatnot, but they split when Milo went to Dublin at eighteen."

Hmm. I frowned. "For something that's been over, what, nine years, you think she wouldn't be so hostile towards me."

Rose shrugged. "I dunno what's goin' through her head. I'm not really friends with her, aye? I'm Muriel's friend, not Darcy's."

We ran through the procedure for the wedding. Fortunately, the aisle was fairly short, being a small church, which meant less time for me to trip while people were watching. I considered that a comfort.

The rehearsal dinner was held afterwards, at a restaurant near the hotel where we were staying for the next two nights. There weren't any hotels in Glencullen itself, so we had a hotel in Enniskerry, in the next county over, a journey of all of five or so miles. They served drinks before dinner; while I didn't have anything alcoholic, I stuck around for the conversation.

Muriel introduced me to her grandparents, Grady and Maureen Hennessy, and to her soon-to-be in-laws, Aidan and Kelley O'Donnell. They were very nice, and obviously fond of their future daughter-in-law. I didn't see how they couldn't be; Muriel was just one of those people you couldn't help but like.

Milo's cousin, Mike--technically his mother's cousin, but the age difference was fairly negligible, since Eithne had had the twins at the age of seventeen--had finally arrived from Utah that afternoon, and I greeted him warmly. I liked Mike, who ran a pub forty miles to the north of where Milo and I both lived.

"How are ya findin' Ireland?" the man asked.

"It's amazing. I haven't had much chance to explore, yet, but Milo says he's going to take me down to Glendalough next week."

"Make sure he takes ya to the Brownshill Dolmen," the red-haired man said. "It's a big rock in the middle of a field, but I think you'll like it."

"Oh, that's definitely on the list," I assured him.

"Good. Oh, have ya been t'see the Book of Kells yet?"

I could tell the instant *he* arrived, because every hair on my body stood on end. I'd never felt anything quite like it, and I turned to the source as if drawn, completely forgetting what I'd been saying to Mike.

The man stood near the door, pale blonde hair carefully styled. He could have been anywhere between thirty and fifty, one of those faces that managed to be worn and lived-in and youthful all at once. He wore a suit, obviously tailored specifically for him, because he was tall. I wouldn't say he was seven feet tall, not quite that gigantic, but he was taller than Milo, and big. Not an ounce of it was fat.

Those of us sensitive to it all turned like compass points to north. He sauntered in, casual as can be, and I could hear Eithne gasp behind me as she finally noticed.

Lugh Lambfadha, *Tuatha Dé Danann* and reputed God of Light, smiled wryly as a ripple went through the room. He glanced at me, briefly, and I saw with a jolt of clarity that his eyes were the same disturbing green as his offspring. Then he moved past me and the spell that had held me rooted was broken.

I excused myself from Mike and made a beeline for Milo, who stood next to his sister, both of them gaping at their estranged sire. And there was no mistaking who he was. The resemblance to the twins, despite their hair, was too strong to deny. I prodded Milo in the side and hugged his arm, so that he couldn't do anything rash. He didn't have the warmest, fuzziest feelings towards the man approaching, and I didn't blame him.

Muriel, standing by her mother, was staring at her estranged father with huge eyes, her face pale and tight. Eithne looked just as shell-shocked. I thought the guy had a lot of nerve, showing up without any sort of notice at his daughter's rehearsal dinner. Milo and Mike both stepped into Lugh's path before he could get to Muriel. Belated, Quinn realized what was going on and joined them.

I sighed and put myself between Milo and his father. "Don't make a scene," I hissed to the group at large. "This is Muriel's wedding rehearsal, not a Sharks and Jets brawl."

Lugh turned that alien gaze from his son to me. I felt dwarfed next to him, and wondered just what the hell I was doing, challenging a freaking *god*. "So you're the witch my son is dating," he said. His voice was a deep rumble, like distant thunder on a warm summer night.

"I'm not a witch," I said automatically. To me, witches were practitioners of Wicca, like my best friend Maegan. What *I* was definitely didn't fall into the same category.

The corner of Lugh's mouth lifted in a smile eerily similar to his son's. "*Cailleach*, then," he said. He looked to his son. "Milo."

"Lugh," my boyfriend replied tersely. "What are ya doin' here?"

Not the friendliest of first words ever, I thought.

"That's no way to greet your father," the *Tuatha Dé Danann* responded.

"Some father you've been."

"Stop," I said. "Not the time. I don't care who you are, Lugh, I happen to like Muriel and if you make her cry, I'll kick you in the 'nads."

Mike laughed. "Marry this one, Milo."

Lugh inclined his head, acknowledging my words. "I've come t'meet my children, that's all."

With a sigh, I stepped aside and let Milo take over. Mike and I watched as Lugh introduced himself to Quinn, then went over and spoke to Muriel.

"So that's what a god looks like, eh?" Mike whispered. "I thought he'd be more . . . glowy."

I laughed.

Darcy sauntered over, drink in hand. "Who's that guy?"

"Milo and Muriel's dad," I said. "His name is Lugh."

She turned dark eyes my way and blinked. "How come *you* know that, an' I don't?"

"Because Milo told me?" I shrugged. "I *do* happen to be his girlfriend."

"I *was* his girlfriend, for four years, an' he didn't tell me anything about his father. What makes you so special, that he'd tell you? He hasn't known ya very long."

Mike cleared his throat. "I'll just, uh . . . be over at the bar, aye?"

I wished he wouldn't go and leave me with Darcy, but he went anyway. "Look, Darcy, whatever happened between you two is just that, between you. I do know that Milo didn't know his dad's name until shortly before he met me, otherwise he probably *would* have told you. But as for what's between me and Milo? As I said, that's between *me* and *Milo*, not you."

I stomped away from her, to join Milo. His father was speaking in a low voice to Muriel and she was shaking her head. Eithne put herself between Lugh and their daughter and said, as I reached them, "I think it's best ya go, Lugh. Please."

A muscle tightened in his jaw, and he nodded once, tightly, then turned on his heel and left. We all watched him leave, then I turned to Milo.

"Everything okay?" I asked.

"Fine. We're all caught up on the subject o' my father," he murmured. "Includin' Quinn."

I looked at the groom, and he was a little pale behind his glasses, but the loving hand resting on Muriel's shoulder said he wasn't calling anything off, Celtic god father-in-law or no.

I sat with Milo at dinner, to the obvious displeasure of Darcy. I had it pretty well figured out that she'd assumed being Maid of Honor to his Best Man would give her a second shot at him, and my presence was a kink in her plan. Milo seemed oblivious, and I wasn't entirely sure how to handle Darcy's thinly-veiled remarks and dark looks.

Finally, I nudged Milo in the side. "Can I talk to you for a minute?"

"Sure."

We went out into the hotel's lobby. He checked to make sure Lugh wasn't loitering outside, then turned to me. "What's up?"

"Darcy's harassing me."

Milo made a face. "Don't drag me inta that."

"Milo, she's- Look. I know you two had a thing, and were together for a while. But I am your girlfriend, and she's making my life really miserable. She was terrible during the rehearsal and tried to trip me. She keeps making snide remarks to me," I told him. I crossed my arms and stared at him. "Dropping hints that she thinks I'm an ignorant, stick-in-the-mud American."

Milo sighed. "Just ignore her, Peyton. She's jealous, is all. A few more days an' she'll be outta yer hair."

"So, what, you're just going to *let* her treat me like crap?"

"Peyton, she's me sister's best friend and Maid of Honor. What do ya want me t'do, cause a big scene an' make her walk out?"

I shook my head. "No. Not at all. I just want my boyfriend to stick up for me."

"You're a big girl, can't ya tell her off yerself?"

My mouth dropped open. For several seconds, I floundered for words, then gave up and spat out,

"So much for chivalry!"

I stormed for the door.

"Stupid, pigheaded Irishman!" I muttered under my breath as I stomped out of the restaurant. It was a bit chilly and I pulled my wrap tighter around my shoulders with one hand, gesturing in irritation with the other. "Bloody-minded, chauvinistic jerk!"

Ranting at the not-present Milo helped to cool my ire a bit. The stomping and flailing did a little more, however, and it wasn't too long before I was able to stop and actually consider what he'd said. Okay, so maybe I was letting Darcy get to me unduly. I'd never been in this position before, though, where the ex was harassing me and my boyfriend was essentially letting her. The only time I'd ever dealt with anything like this was when Rob had died and his former girlfriend, the one he'd left me for, had come to me for help. But I'd only met her once and then she'd been murdered. The lessons I might have learned there didn't apply in this situation.

And Milo was mine, darn it. Wasn't I allowed to feel upset that his ex-girlfriend was being a pest and nasty to me? Men!

I sighed and shivered, realizing that in my anger, I hadn't been paying attention to my surroundings. It was early evening, and I had no freaking clue where I was. I was completely lost, and my cell phone didn't have reception here in Podunk, Ireland. Why it was even taking up space in my handbag, I had no idea. Oh, right, I was addicted to Bejeweled.

"Brilliant," I groaned, and slapped a hand to my eyes.

I'd wandered down a cute little alley between two cottages, and I took a look around, not entirely certain which direction I'd come from. It all looked the same to me: quaint and green.

You're really stupid, my Inner Voice told me.

"Shut up," I told it.

I headed back down the alley, hoping that something would begin to look familiar. I hadn't taken more than three steps before my heel caught between two atmospheric cobblestones and I wobbled. I dropped my purse, grabbed the nearest fencepost, and pivoted on my heel, almost falling over in the process.

When I came to a stop, I had my left leg stuck to the knee in a rosebush. After I'd finished yelping, I considered my predicament. The thorns were thoroughly snagged in my pantyhose, effectively stapling me to the bush. Naturally, I was wearing the full hose, and not the thigh-highs I'd saved for the wedding itself.

I glanced surreptitiously around. Seeing no one, I heaved a sigh and hiked my skirt up with my free hand, the other wrapped firmly around the fence post to keep my balance.

Two nuns chose that very moment to walk past down the street. They didn't see me immediately. It took about ten seconds for them to take in the sight of me standing on one leg, with my skirt up to my hip and the other leg in some stranger's garden.

"It isn't what it looks like," I said weakly.

The two women, obviously scandalized, turned and hurried in the opposite direction. I didn't catch all of their hushed comments, but what I heard had something to do with Americans with no sense of decency.

I thunked my head down on the fence post and swore under my breath. I braced myself on the post and yanked my leg out of the rose bush. My nylons tore and blood trickled down my leg from the dozens of little scratches—some not so little—I'd just earned myself. I yelped and whimpered, and nearly fell on my butt.

Milo found me roughly five minutes later, walking in stocking feet down the road, shoes in hand. I had stray rose petals in my hair and stuck to my skirt, and one leg was mostly bare, save for the bloody shreds of my pantyhose.

He stopped, hands shoved in his pants pockets, and eyed me up and down for a long moment. He apparently decided not to voice whatever comment came to mind first, and instead asked, "Do I *want* to know, *cailín*?"

"I had an argument with a rose bush. The rose bush won."

I didn't mention the nuns.

***

We didn't go back to the restaurant, instead going up to his room at the hotel. Milo pulled me over to sit on the bed, which was pretty much the only available surface. I was too irritated with him, still, to let thoughts of how private we had things invade my mind.

"I'm sorry," he said. "I didn't mean t'make ya feel like I . . . don't care or that I don't support ya. I do. I just don't wanna make things difficult wi' my sister, aye? Darcy's her best friend, an' it's been awkward enough that I used t'date her. I don't wanna make things outright hostile."

I leaned my head against his shoulder. "I know. I'm just insecure about this. Us. My last boyfriend left me and then died. I don't think I could stand it if-"

There was no way I was going to be able to finish that sentence. Milo knew what I meant, though, and he tipped my chin up with a finger.

"Peyton," he said softly. "I'm not leavin' ya. Who was it I brought five thousand miles t'meet my family?"

"Me," I whispered.

"Aye. That tell ya anything?"

"Um."

He shook his head and rolled his eyes heavenward. "It *should* tell ya that I love you."

I ducked my head, fighting the urge to cry. It was a silly, girlish reaction, but Rob had never said it to me. Milo had said it before, in a way, but not in those precise, three little words. I'd longed to hear them.

He sighed and ran his big hands over my hair. "Ah, *cailín*. Please tell me you're not cryin'."

I huffed a laugh and quickly dashed away a few tears. "No, I'm not. It's just been a stressful day."

Reaching up, I cupped his face in my hands.

I'd always had such a hard time letting people in and telling them how I felt. The depth of my feelings for Milo scared me sometimes: fear at letting him get that close and then losing him, fear of making myself vulnerable. Fear of failing him somehow.

I licked my lips. Those inhumanly green eyes seemed to see straight to my soul, making it impossible to look away. "Me, too," I said, and it came out as a croak. Way to go, self. Clearing my throat, I tried again. "I love you, too."

He bent his head and pressed his lips to my forehead. "I know."

I giggled suddenly. "You get frozen in carbonite now and I'll kick your butt."

Milo snorted. He pulled me with him as he moved to recline on the bed. I rested my head on his shoulder, tucked against his side. It was nice to be held like this.

Naturally, I had to go and ruin the mood by blurting, "Did you sleep with her?"

"Who?"

"Darcy."

Milo turned to his side and half-rose, hand braced on the bed. He eyed me skeptically. "D'you *really* want me t'answer that?"

"That right there told me you did," I responded. "Maybe I'm masochistic, but I need to hear it."

He closed his eyes and sighed. "What d'you think, *cailín*? We dated four years, an' I'm no saint. Yeah, she an' I, uh . . ."

Awkward.

"I don't want details. I just needed to know . . . what I'm up against."

Milo pulled me close again and pressed his lips to the top of my head. "Far as I'm concerned, nothin'. You're mine an' I'm yours. Got it?"

I sighed. "Got it."

CHAPTER SIX

Dawn came far too early for my tastes. I forced myself out of bed to attend the bridesmaids' breakfast. Once again, Ciara was absent.

"Oh, she'll be here later," Darcy said. "Probably. She works late. And I wouldn't put it past her to have met a fella."

Muriel shook her head. "Ciara will be here. She may be *late*, but she'll be here."

Once we'd eaten, we headed off to a nearby styling salon. Muriel didn't have a curling iron, since her hair was naturally that way. I resigned myself to letting a stylist do it. I came out of the place with my dark blonde hair artfully coiffed, my hat pinned on. It was silly to be in jeans and my pajama top, with my hair and makeup done and a fascinator on my head. I felt much better once I had my gown on. I was definitely taller in the teal and black shoes, though everyone else still towered over me. And here I'd been told the Irish were short. Ha!

When I met Milo at the church, having gone in the car with Rose and Nell, he let out a low whistle. I took perverse pleasure in seeing Darcy turn green with envy when Milo trailed a finger along the lace at the neckline of my dress, pausing maybe a little too long at my cleavage.

"Nice dress," he said. He stooped to kiss me briefly, careful not to smudge the lipstick. I was wearing the one he'd helped pick. "Ya look gorgeous, *cailín*. I like the hat."

"Thanks. You look pretty spiffy yourself." I smoothed a hand over his green waistcoat, an exact shade to match his eyes. "I like you in a tux. I'll have to think of more ways to get you into one."

And one day, maybe, *out* of it.

Milo turned his attention to the arriving bride. He looked floored at the sight of his twin in all her finery, her hair piled up in a mass of curls, her veil already in place. Muriel hadn't opted for a plain-white gown, and I agreed with her choice. She didn't have that demure of a personality. This one had pale washes of blue, green, pink, and purple on the bodice, with matching flowers trailing down one side of the skirt. It was sleeveless, but like me, she had on a lace jacket to cover her shoulders while we were in the church.

"You're beautiful," Milo told his sister. "You're gonna knock Quinn's socks off, ya know."

She grinned and kissed his cheek through the veil. "You're the best brother I could have, Milo. I love ya."

After that, we all lined up. Milo went inside to stand with Quinn and I took my place just ahead of the flower girl and the ringbearer, two adorable kids from Quinn's side. Ciara was still nowhere to be seen. Muriel didn't seem too bothered, but she was preoccupied by other things: namely, getting married.

As Maid of Honor, Darcy went up the aisle first, followed by Nell, Rose, and then me. I saw Milo standing beside Quinn, and in a sudden flash, for a moment I saw their positions reversed, Quinn as best man, and Milo waiting for *me*.

I stumbled for the briefest moment, regained my footing, and continued up the aisle. Darcy leaned past the other bridesmaids and hissed, "Spaz." I ignored her. I was too busy watching *her* best friend walk up the aisle on the arm of her grandfather. I didn't blame Muriel for not having Lugh escort her; after all, she'd just met the man.

When they reached the front, I caught Milo's eye and he smiled.

Some of the ceremony was in Latin. I'd never been to a Catholic wedding before. It was basically Mass with a wedding in the middle. The censer gave me a headache, but I managed to stay there through the entire thing.

After the ceremony, there was no particular order to our departure after the bride and groom.

Milo took my arm, which obviously miffed Darcy. There was a luncheon after the wedding, outdoors at Quinn's parents' home. Since seating wasn't formal like it would be at the reception, Milo and I sat with his grandparents. I hadn't spoken with them much the night before, so this would be nice, I hoped.

Milo's grandmother was taller than me by a few inches, but virtually petite next to her grandchildren. I sat beside her at the table and she patted my hand.

"It's so wonderful to put a face to the name," Maureen said. Her salt-and-pepper hair was straight; the curls came from her husband, whose pate was mostly bald but held a silvery hint of the same hair Milo and Muriel sported. "How are you finding Ireland? A bit slow compared to America, I'd say."

"Oh, Ireland is wonderful," I assured her. "It's definitely slower, especially the speed limits, but I think it's great. And the land's so pretty. It's mostly desert where I come from, though we've got some trees and stuff in the city itself."

She asked me questions about Utah; her husband sat in silence, watching the festivities with a rather neutral expression. He was difficult to read, and something told me I didn't really want to try.

Milo came over and asked if I'd do him a favor. "Sure," I replied. "What is it?"

He merely gestured for me to follow, and I did. His mother's car was waiting in the lot, and my boyfriend held the passenger door for me. We drove to the hotel, where the reception was being set up in the ballroom. I nearly collided with a man carrying a large arrangement of flowers; I dimly recognized him as the florist from earlier, back to set up for the reception. Must be one heck of a refrigerated truck to keep those things fresh over hours. Showed how little I knew about this stuff.

Once in the ballroom, I saw immediately what Milo needed help with. When he'd moved to the US, he'd brought his acoustic guitar and left his electric in Donegal, with his mother. Eithne had brought that instrument with her when she'd driven down to Dublin. Milo was going to sing for his sister's first dance at the reception, which I thought was beyond sweet.

I helped Milo and a guy named Angus Fitzgerald set up. Angus was Milo's other best friend, the one that had converted my boyfriend to Druidism when they were fourteen. I'd been curious about him ever since Milo had told me.

I hadn't really had a chance to meet Angus before the wedding started. Milo handled the introductions as I untangled guitar cords.

"Pleased t'meetcha," the thin blonde man said. He was one of those guys with blonde hair and a red beard. "Milo says ya work at a Wiccan shop. Nice to meet another practitioner, wi' all these Catholics around."

"Oh, I don't practice," I said. "I'm Christian, just not Catholic."

A change immediately went over Angus. He visibly shut down, the smile vanishing, and he turned a look at Milo.

"What?" my boyfriend asked. He'd missed the conversation, preoccupied with tuning his guitar.

"Later," Angus snapped.

Huh. Well, that was weird.

Milo handed me his guitar. "You said ya play?" It was really more of a statement than a question.

I shrugged. "I haven't picked up either of mine since I broke my wrist. But I can give it a shot."

Taking the instrument, feeling a little silly standing there in my fancy dress with the strap slung over my head, I tested a few notes. I had an electric bass and an acoustic guitar back home; the former I'd received as a Christmas present in high school, the latter I'd purchased online more recently but hadn't had much success with.

I strummed a few measures of a Howie Day song, then winced. "I need to build my strength back up in this hand."

Milo took the guitar back, and set it aside, before he caught my hand and lightly massaged my wrist. "You want guitar lessons?" he asked. "I know ye're self-taught."

"Sure."

He kissed my palm. Behind him, I noted Angus glaring at me.

Darcy arrived, with Rose. She hesitated in the doorway for a moment when she saw me and Milo together, but squared her shoulders and glided over.

"You're playing for Muriel and Quinn's dance?" she asked, though she obviously already knew. "That's sweet of ya. What are ya playin'?"

"'Everything I Do'," Milo responded.

She blinked.

"Bryan Adams song," I supplied. "One of my favorites, too."

Milo smiled at me.

Darcy turned those big, doe-like brown eyes at me. "Peyton, would ya be a help an' supervise the guestbook tonight?"

"Sorry," I replied, just as fake-sweet. "I'm Milo's plus-one. I'm flattered you'd trust me with such an *important* job, but I'm afraid that tonight, I'm pretty much decorative, not functional."

My boyfriend snorted a laugh. "Leave 'er alone, Darce. Aye?"

Defeated, she stomped off in her four-inch heels to regroup.

"What did you ever see in her?" I asked.

Milo's face turned pink. "Not much. I was a teenager an' she was easy."

I smacked his arm and we went back to setting up.

***

Muriel had been savvier than I'd expected; she hadn't seated Darcy next to Milo at all. Instead, the place card at dinner bore my name.

"She's hoping we're headed for the altar," I told Milo as we sat down. I would have been lying if I said all this wedding stuff hadn't brought up thoughts of the same in my own mind.

"Yeah, pretty obvious about it, too." He held my chair for me, then took his seat.

There were toasts. Mercifully, I didn't have to give one. I didn't know the bride or the groom well enough to offer one, and I was horrible at giving speeches. The dead I can deal with. I can even, apparently, tell a god where to stuff it. Stand in front of a group of people I don't know and talk? No way, no how.

Once the dinner was cleared away, the reception began. I didn't know what traditions were held here in Ireland, regarding weddings. Back home in Utah, reception lines were popular. Muriel didn't have one, which I was immensely relieved to see, because as one of the wedding party, I'd have had to stood and shake hands with strangers. My shielding was already taxed just from the number of people in attendance. Having to touch them would have broken it completely.

For the bride and groom's first dance, Milo sang. I could never get enough of hearing him. One of our first dates had been to an open mic night at his cousin's pub in Salt Lake City, and I had fond memories of that.

It was obvious, watching Muriel and Quinn dance, that they were so in love. They only had eyes for each other, and I envied them having that. Not that I wasn't happy with Milo. But the security of being husband and wife? That was something I wanted.

The song finished and Milo bowed and grinned at the scattered applause. Then he put down the guitar and bounded across the dance floor to me. Behind him, Angus gave me a dirty look and pointedly turned his back to us.

"Now the DJ takes over," Milo said, oblivious to his friend's odd behavior, "and I get to dance with my girl."

He spun me around and I laughed as I wobbled on my heels. With a big grin, Milo ducked his head and kissed me. When we separated, I murmured, "Darcy is glaring."

Milo made a suggestion about what Darcy could do with herself, one I didn't think was anatomically possible. I laughed and kissed him again.

"Mm. I can't seem to keep my hands off you," I told him.

"That's fine wi' me."

"Yeah, I'll bet." I laughed. "I'm gonna go ditch this hat in my room. I'll be right back."

CHAPTER SEVEN

Lugh and a small group of women arrived about halfway through the reception. I had just returned from the facilities when I saw them. One of them, a redhead, slipped into the general crowd. Three of the women were nearly identical, at least in the face. I stared openly for a long moment, wondering if they were one of the triple goddesses.

They noticed me and gestured to themselves, before the one with the pixie cut dragged the other two my way. I resigned myself to speaking to them, since there was no feasible way I could take off.

"Hullo!" she said. She was rather perky and bright. "I'm Erin. These are my sisters, Bonnie an' Fohla. You're the *cailleach*?"

"Um. I guess that's what they're calling me," I said weakly. I looked for Milo, but he was talking to Quinn across the room.

Bonnie, the one with a shoulder-length bob of glossy, medium-brown hair, jabbed her sister in the ribs. "Lugh was tellin' us about you, an' we had to meet ya."

"Oh. Um. Hi."

The third sister, whom I took to be Fohla, had ankle-length hair that she wore in a braid. She rolled her eyes at her sisters. "You're scarin' the human," she said. "I'm goin' to introduce meself t'the bride. Try not t'mess with her head too much, aye?"

Erin looked abashed. "Sorry. It's been a while since we've been, uh, outside. Lugh says your name is Peyton."

I nodded. "Peyton Reynolds. And I'm not a witch. I'm a psychic."

"What's the difference?" Bonnie asked.

That was probably a good question, at least to them. "I'm not a pagan, for one? I have visions and I talk to the dead, but I don't cast spells and things like that."

"Ah, I see." Erin nodded and nudged Bonnie. "Ooh, there's Lugh's boy. Let's go say hi. Nice t'meet you, Peyton!"

They scurried off. I stood for a moment in silence, blinking as I gathered my thoughts. With a sigh, I resigned myself to the fact that my life was never, ever going to be normal.

***

While Milo danced with his sister, I took the opportunity to sit down with some punch and a cookie. Pardon me. *Biscuit.* I was halfway through when a young man approached me, dropping into the closest available chair.

"Hi," he said, offering a hand. "Brendan, cousin of Muriel's."

I was usually reluctant to shake hands with people, but it was difficult to avoid at a wedding, especially with so many friendly guests. I hadn't been able to avoid all the physical contact like I'd been hoping earlier. I shook his for good measure.

"Peyton Reynolds," I said.

Brendan smiled. He was good looking in a lean manner, with a narrow face, handsome in that Black Irish way: olive complexion, short and straight black hair that fell in his dark eyes. His nose was thin and long, but it didn't detract from the rest of his features. I didn't see much of a resemblance between Milo and this cousin, other than hair color, and maybe the jawline. They both had strong jaws.

"Peyton," he repeated. "You been in Ireland long, Peyton?"

I shook my head. "Just a few days. My boyfriend is the bride's brother and the groom's best man."

"Ah. My cousin Milo. He's always had a way wi' da ladies." Brendan's accent was more nasal and sharper than my sweetie's; I didn't know enough about regional dialects to place where he'd grown up.

I noticed Milo had finished dancing and was headed my way. Brendan rose with surprising alacrity and murmured, "Lovely meetin' ya, Peyton." Then he was gone.

"Who was that?" Milo asked as he joined me.

"Your cousin Brendan," I informed him. "Seems like a nice guy."

My boyfriend frowned and looked off in the direction Brendan had gone.

"What?" I asked, an uneasy feeling creeping over me the longer he didn't speak.

"I don't *have* a cousin named Brendan."

***

Milo conferred with his mother, then returned with his father to the table I'd claimed. I was a little surprised to see Lugh and Milo in each other's company.

"What'd he look like?" Lugh demanded.

"Brendan? Um. Shorter than Milo, about six-foot-one? Dark hair, somewhat swarthy complexion, dark eyes, on the thin side."

"Mam says I definitely don't have a cousin named Brendan on her side," Milo said. "It's just her an' Mike, wi' her brother gone. Mike's still single, no kids."

"Might be from my side," Lugh admitted. "Danu knows we been breedin' right and left. Not recently, though. Only ones in two centuries are my son an' daughter."

My brain shied away from that statement. Six months into the relationship, and it was still weird to acknowledge that my sweetie was less than human.

The huge blonde glowered for a moment

before shaking his head. "I'm goin' to speak with Brigit. She always knows when someone's born."

I followed his gaze to the stunning redhead in the green sequined dress speaking with Milo's mother, the woman I'd noticed prior to being accosted by Erin and Bonnie. Lugh left us and I asked Milo, "Who's Brigit?"

He sighed. "Goddess of Fertility. One of 'em, anyway."

"Oh." No wonder Lugh had looked annoyed; there was a huge feud between her family and his, something about her kids killing Lugh's father . . .? I shrugged it off; their backgrounds were as convoluted as their genetics.

After we'd all waved the happy couple off, I helped Eithne with the clearing up, until she shooed me away with a, "You're a guest, Peyton. Go enjoy the music for a bit before the DJ shuts down."

I knew better than to argue; I knew full well that I was more of a hindrance sometimes than a help. The DJ still had music going and quite a few guests were occupied on the floor. Milo'd gone off to help with something or other, so I was by myself for the present.

Finally able to pry off my shoes, I hobbled over on sore feet over to the table where I'd been sitting with Milo. It had been very nice of Muriel to include me at the family's table, letting me sit with my boyfriend instead of across the room. I put my shoes on the chair that already held my handbag and my wrap.

I sighed, flexing my toes to get some proper feeling in them. Tired as I was from the long day, I really hoped Milo didn't have anything planned for the next day. We were going to be here for another week, and I needed some rest. Weddings can be exhausting.

Suddenly, arms enveloped me from behind. I jumped a little, even as I realized it had to be Milo: no one else here was as big, his father excluded, and Lugh wasn't about to hug me.

Milo dropped a kiss on the top of my head. "We can get outta here if ya like," he murmured. "Mam said as much."

"Yeah," I said. "Let's do that."

***

My room at the hotel was down a curved set of stairs, in a little room with a pointed arch door and stone walls, barely large enough for the full-sized bed and a granite shelf that functioned as a desk. The bed was opposite a deep window; a small alcove beside the bed held a candle that lit the room.

I dropped my shoes by the foot of the bed and sat on the mattress. Milo crouched by my feet and took one in his large hands.

"I don't understand why women wear heels," he said, as he pressed his thumbs into the ball of my foot.

"You only say that because you're not a foot shorter than me," I told him. "If you were in my place, you wouldn't wonder."

He reached over and picked up one of my discarded heels, holding it up. "Aye, but do ya need four-inch ones?"

"I'm five-two, Milo. You're six-four. Even *with* the heels, I don't reach your chin."

Milo moved to sit beside me on the bed. "I know how we can be more even."

"Yeah?"

He crooked a finger and then pulled me to him. I straddled his lap, my skirt bunching up around my thighs. Sitting there did help the height difference, but it made me very aware of how alone and how very close we were.

His hands slid into my hair as he leaned in to kiss me. I flattened my hands on his broad chest and sighed as I closed my eyes. I wiggled closer and cupped his face in my palms. He dropped his hands to my knees to give me the access.

I lightly bit his bottom lip, tugging at it with my teeth. Milo's hands moved from my knees and slid up my thighs, under the satin and lace of my skirt. His fingers stopped and his breath hitched when he reached the tops of my stockings and my garter belt. His reaction was immediate and obvious, with me in his lap.

I sucked in a sharp breath. Milo groaned and abruptly shifted, flipping me onto my back. His weight pressed me into the bed, heavy and warm and undeniably male. A very, very interested male. My heart began pounding as his lips slid from my mouth, across my jaw, and down my neck.

He was more experienced than I was, since I'd never gone past some lingering kisses with my ex. Milo and I hadn't even gone *this* far, largely because my mother the ghost could intrude on us at any time, and she would have really disapproved.

But we were a continent and an ocean away, and I was feeling reckless.

"*Cailín*," he rasped. "I want ya."

It was hard to think of why we shouldn't. I really wanted to, and I wasn't even sure I would regret it later. This felt so right. Milo moved against me and I moaned, wrapping my legs around his hips.

He buried his face against my neck. "Make me stop, Peyton, or I won't."

I tangled my fingers in his hair and tipped my head back. Truthfully, I didn't want him to stop. Being wanted was something I'd craved for so long. Unable to connect with others out of fear of my clairvoyance until I'd met Milo, knowing how he felt about me was intoxicating.

"Milo," I began, and opened my eyes.

A young woman stood by the bed, staring down at us with vacant eye sockets. Black blood dripped from the stab wounds in her chest and her dark hair seemed to float behind her. I screamed.

Startled by my shriek, Milo fell off the bed, which abruptly put an end to things. He blinked at the apparition for a moment, before she vanished into thin air.

I was hyperventilating, and had crawled backwards to huddle against the wall. "Tha- That- I've never- What-"

Milo returned to the bed and pulled me into his arms. "Hush, *cailín*. S'alright. Just a ghostie. They come w' buildin's old as this one."

"I've never seen one that looked like that," I squeaked. "She had no eyes!"

He ran his fingers through my hair, which I'll

admit I found comforting. "Didn't ya say you saw what's-her-name, the queen w'no head?"

"Yeah, but that's just Anne. It isn't . . . bloody." I drew a shaky breath and pried my fingers out of his dress shirt. "I've never seen that kind of ghost before."

Milo kissed my temple. "It's scary, but you'll live. Guess she thought we needed t'cool down."

I had to laugh a little at that. "Maybe."

He laced his fingers through mine. "You know I wouldn't pressure ya into anything, right?"

I nodded. Belatedly, I realized that my skirt was pretty much a belt at this point. I flushed and yanked it back down. He'd looked, of course he had, but had the tact not to mention it.

Milo cupped the back of my head and kissed me softly. "I'll let ya get some sleep. Best if I leave now, anyway."

He excused himself and I flopped on the bed with a dejected sigh.

***

I woke late the next morning, barely in time to make checkout. We were going to be house-sitting for Muriel and Quinn while they were in Paris, so I hadn't brought more than a change of clothes with me, anyway.

I was in the process of stowing away my gown when someone pounded on the door.

"Peyton!" Milo hollered through the panel. "Open up! We need ya."

I smoothed my hair as I went to answer it,

hoping I didn't look as tired as I felt. Soon as I opened it, Milo pushed through, looking just as tired and a lot more worried.

"What's wrong?" I asked, alarm replacing my laconic mood. "Has something happened?"

"Aye, somethin' happened," he said, and reached out to hug me tightly. "Remember how Ciara didn't show for the wedding? Well, they found her this mornin'."

I took it from his tone that she hadn't been found in good health. "Tell me."

His expression turned grim. "You remember that ghost we saw last night, one that interrupted us?"

The sinking feeling made me go sit on the bed. "Don't tell me that was her."

His silence was answer enough. I swore.

There was another knock at the open door, this one more polite. We both looked over to see one of Milo's paternal relatives there. I tried to remember if it was Bonnie or Erin; I knew it wasn't Fohla, because that one had ankle-length hair and this triplet had a pixie cut.

"Good, ye're awake," she said without preamble. "Lugh's puttin' on a show in the drawing room."

CHAPTER EIGHT

I gathered the rest of my things and we went up the stairs to the little hotel's drawing room. Lugh paced before the gathering, tall and regal and frightening in his fury. I leaned towards the triplet that had fetched us.

"Why's he so angry?" I asked.

Lugh heard me and turned, waving a hand at me. "I'm angry because someone's murdered a girl close t'my daughter, an' sacrificed her as well."

Oh . . . kaaaay. I thought it was a little presumptuous of him to be angry about the feelings of a daughter he'd just barely met, but then, I was angry for Muriel, too, and I'd known her only fractionally longer. "What do you mean?" I found myself asking. "Sacrificed?"

He looked from me to Milo, asking his son, "Does she not know?"

"*I* barely know what you're blatherin' about," my boyfriend said.

Abruptly, the big man sat down on a comically-small chair and ran long fingers through his blonde hair. "The girl, Ciara. The Gardai say that she was found with a garrote round her neck, her eyes cut out. An' she was stuffed in a wicker chest that the fool tried ta burn. Eriu and I went t'check it out."

Oh, right. The pixie-cut triplet had introduced herself as Erin, and the one with the shoulder-length shag was Banba, or as she'd asked me to call her, Bonnie. I had to admit, I liked the sisters so far. I still wasn't sure what to make of Brigit.

"And it's a sacrifice how?" Milo inquired. "To whom?"

"Dunno," Erin said. "Whoever it was didn't finish the ritual, but human sacrifice? No one's done that in centuries."

I swallowed hard. Muriel was going to be devastated. I remembered Ciara as a sweet but ditzy brunette, who hadn't been able to hold her liquor and who'd been described as something of a flake. "When was she killed?"

They all turned to look at me. I cleared my throat and went on. "I mean, did she die last night, or before?"

Erin lifted one shoulder. "We don't know yet."

I looked to Milo. "Has anyone told Muriel yet?"

"No," he said. "We've only just found out,

aye? An' she and Quinn are on their way to France already."

"She'll never forgive you if you don't tell her quick," I said, and he nodded before I'd finished speaking.

"I told Quinn. Well, I left a message on his phone, askin' him to call me when they land in Paris." Milo dragged a hand through his hair. It was probably wrong of me to notice how good he looked in his jeans and dark blue sweater.

Eithne came into the room, her overnight bag in hand. "I hear a commotion?"

Milo told his mother what had happened. She sat in one of the poufy chairs and pressed one hand to her cheek. "Oh, no."

We were soon joined by the rest of the still-lingering wedding party, and they were rapidly filled in on news of Ciara's death, though not on the how of it. They were the mundanes of the group and didn't necessarily need to know everything.

The hotel staff was understanding over the horrible turn of events and didn't charge anyone extra even though we were a bit late checking out. Milo had Quinn's car, full of presents, and I drove back to Muriel and Quinn's with his mother. We were all quiet on the drive.

Milo's phone rang as we were taking our things into the house. I assisted Eithne with getting presents and things out of the vehicles while Milo delivered the bad news to his sister.

"Quinn's talked her inta stayin' in Paris," Milo told us once he'd hung up and joined us in the kitchen for the tea his mother had prepared. "She's upset, naturally, but what could she do here?"

"Right," Eithne said. She sighed. "Such a shame. I didn't know Ciara, but . . ."

"It still sucks," I said. I thought back to the ghost that had interrupted us the night before and I shuddered. "I wonder if . . ."

When I trailed off, Milo set down his mug and reached across the table to take my hand. "Wonder what, *cailín*?"

Suddenly uncomfortable with everything, I rolled my shoulders restlessly. "I keep wondering if she died the night of the bachelorette party, or if it happened last night."

At Eithne's inquiring expression, I briefly explained seeing Ciara the night before. "Or, well, really early this morning, I guess, but whatever. I'm inclined to think it was last night. Otherwise, I think she would have appeared sooner."

"Logical way to see it," Eithne said.

I got up to put my mug in the sink, and there was a knock at the front door. Since I was the one up, I went to answer it.

Lugh stood at the door, in what he probably viewed as casual clothing: dark grey slacks, black loafers, and a long-sleeved black tee that looked to be made of cashmere. He had his blonde hair tailed at the nape of his neck. Behind him, at the curb, a sleek, pewter Mercedes Benz took up space between a dinky Peugeot that had seen better days, and the O'Donnells' Volkswagen sedan. The car, and Lugh, were completely out of place in this neighborhood.

"Oh," I said. "Hi."

"May I come in?"

I mentally debated it. Muriel was livid at her father, but she also wasn't here. Still, it was her house.

Milo saved me from having to make the choice by appearing behind me and saying, "Let him in, Peyton."

I stepped back and granted the god entrance. He stepped past me and I shut the door, but not before having a good look outside to see if Hellfire was raining down. Nope, just the typical Irish drizzle. So far, so good.

Eithne was not pleased to see her estranged lover, evident by the tight set of her mouth, but she stayed civil as she greeted Lugh with reserve. Even though I wasn't a fan of tea, I retrieved my mug from the counter where I'd set it and got another cupful, mostly as something to do. The atmosphere in the little kitchen was suddenly tense and cloying.

"I realize I'm not welcome," Lugh said after a long moment. "And you're justified in that. But at the moment, I happen to be High King and this needs addressing."

"Really?" I blurted. "High King of what? All of Ireland, or the fairies?"

Everyone looked at me, and I instantly flushed, clamming up. Milo winked at me, amused, but I was still embarrassed.

"The *Tuatha Dé Danann*," Lugh clarified. "But I have . . . I believe the term you would know is conservatorship? There are a group of us that have taken an interest in protecting Ireland to the extent we can, without interfering overmuch with the human government."

Toasted

He moved from where he stood in the doorway and took a seat at the table, though no one had offered him one. "We started this after our neglect led to the Famine. Brigit, myself, and a few others still take an interest in our home. A board of directors, if you will, and I would be the . . . CEO."

Well, that was interesting to know. "But that applies how?" I asked. In for a penny, in for a pound, as the saying went. Except they didn't use pounds anymore, they used Euro dollars. Whatever.

Those strange green eyes, familiar to me in Milo's face but alien in Lugh's, met mine. He seemed to weigh his words before speaking.

"I know the murdered girl appeared to you last night," he said at last. "Eriu informed me that she overheard you and my son discussing it when she fetched you this morning. I'm reluctant to put such a burden on you, my dear, but I need you to deal with this."

I had to set the mug down before I dropped it. "You want me to *what*?"

Milo, too, was off-put by this. "You want her to solve this murder? Are you out of your bloody mind?"

It wasn't like I hadn't before, but I'd been dragged into that by my ex and his bimbo of a cheating girlfriend. I was only peripheral to this one, at best.

"Ciara Murphy's spirit appeared to Peyton for a reason," Lugh said, raising a hand to cut off his son's protests. "I know it's a lot to ask, and you're not in Ireland for very long. If necessary, I can handle any difficulties with your airlines, in the event you need to extend your stay. But Brigit agrees with me that we need you."

I looked at Milo. He'd hated my being involved in the investigation of Rob Morris's death six months before, and he'd had a point: I'd nearly ended up killed myself. But how did one refuse a *god*?

Apparently, my boyfriend was thinking the same thing. It didn't help that he was a Druid and had, since the age of fourteen, been worshipping the very deities he'd only recently discovered were actually family. That had to be one heck of a mind-screw.

Milo shrugged, looked unhappy. I sighed.

"Can I have a little time to think about it?" I asked Lugh finally.

The *Tuatha* eyed me in silence for a long moment, then nodded once. "We are, obviously, pressed for time in this, but yes."

He rose from the table, not making eye contact with Eithne even though he'd been in my chair, directly across from her. We let Milo walk him to the door.

"Well," Eithne said, after a minute or so of silence. "The nerve of that man."

"He actually has something of a point," I told her. "I *did* see Ciara's ghost last night. But it's a nasty position he's put me in."

"I don't like it," Milo put in.

I went to him and wrapped my arms tight around his waist. "I know," I said against his chest.

I wanted to say no. I wanted to run back to the States and bury my head. But that felt like a betrayal of Ciara, who had come to *me*. What was I to do?

***

We were left in a strange limbo state after Lugh's visit. It was Sunday, and the original plan had been to just laze around the house and unwind after the festivities, but none of us could do that after learning of Ciara's death.

We decided to go to lunch, since none of us felt like cooking, and we ended up walking to a small restaurant near the house. Lugh's "request" lay heavily on me. I didn't know what to do. I couldn't say no, not really, but could I say yes? Could I do it? I was afraid, and uncertain.

When we returned to the house, a marked police car was parked where Lugh's Mercedes had loitered earlier. It was a white hatchback, decorated in blue and a truly eye-hurting fluorescent yellow. Eithne was worried about this turn of events, but Milo assured her it was likely just procedure, speaking to everyone who'd seen Ciara recently.

Actually, I was probably one of the last few to have seen Ciara alive, but I didn't mention that.

A uniformed officer of *An Garda Síochána* was just coming down the walk as we reached the gate. He tipped his hat to Eithne.

"Evening, mum," he said, and introduced himself as Garda Kevin O'Malley. "I'm looking for Muriel Hennessy and Quinn O'Donnell?"

"They're in France," Eithne said. "On their honeymoon. Can I help you?"

In the end, she invited the man in and offered

him tea. We all sat somewhat nervously in the parlor.

"Detective Inspector Byrne figured as much," the officer confessed. "That we'd missed the happy couple. Would you mind if I let him know you're available to speak to?"

"Go ahead," Milo said. "Best get it over with, anyway."

The officer nodded and gave the detective inspector a call. Seemed a little odd to me, but I had no idea if this was standard police procedure in Ireland, or just a random bit of time-saving footwork on the detective's part. Send a uniform around to question people and not drive around yourself.

We didn't have to wait long for the man himself to arrive. Detective Inspector Cormac Byrne was a tall, thin man in a taupe suit, with a ruddy complexion and auburn hair cut viciously short. He was, he informed us, in charge of Ciara's murder until the National Bureau of Criminal Investigation took over.

Eithne didn't have much to say, as she'd never met Ciara. Milo only had a little to add, but the last time he'd seen Ciara in person had been nearly a year before. I was the one Byrne was most interested in interviewing.

"I'm not really sure what I can tell you," I told the detective. "She was drunk but so were the others. I was Muriel's designated driver, so I didn't have anything, but the others had a lot to drink. She seemed fine when we all parted ways at the last pub. She only had a couple blocks to walk, said I shouldn't put myself out driving her."

"Did you notice anything, any altercations she

had with anyone, or anyone following?"

I shook my head. "Nothing. Actually, she was really popular. I only met her the once, and didn't talk to her much, I'm ashamed to say."

Det. Ins. Byrne left not long after that. I wished I'd had more to tell him, but I just didn't know who would hurt Ciara, or why. Especially to do such a brutal thing to her as cut her eyes out and carve into her chest. Byrne hadn't told us any of those details, but Milo and I had seen her ghost. I knew what had been done.

"Question," I said to Milo, after his mother excused herself to go up to bed.

"What's that?" Milo was in the middle of checking the locks on windows and doors.

"I don't see gory ghosts. It just doesn't happen to me. All that stuff in *The Sixth Sense*, the kid with the back of his head blown off? I don't see that. So why did I see Ciara that way?"

Milo wrapped an arm around my shoulders. "I dunno, *cailín*. I can't answer that. Manannán might be able t'tell ya, but he's not here."

My left eyelid twitched at that. I wondered briefly if I'd ever stop having that kind of reaction to his dad's side of the family. Probably not. "Yeah."

"Maybe, if you see her again, she won't be so . . ." He gestured towards his face.

"I sure hope so."

His hands slid down my back, settling on my hips. "Peyton . . ."

"Yeah?"

"Last night, before she appeared to us . . ."

Right. That. My cheeks flushed just remembering the passion that had flared between us. "What about it?"

"If she hadn't stopped us," he began, then hesitated.

"I dunno," I admitted. "I really don't. I want to. Someday. Just not yet."

He nodded, kissed my forehead. "All right. Figured I'd ask, is all."

We went to our separate rooms. I lay awake for hours, too caught up with questions about Ciara, about the dark-eyed figure I kept seeing in my dreams, and what I was going to do about this turn in my relationship with Milo.

Eventually, I slept, but wasn't any closer to an answer to anything.

CHAPTER NINE

In the morning, after seeing Eithne off on her way back to Donegal, Milo and I drove into Dublin City proper. We left the car at a garage near Grafton Street and wandered up to Trinity College, where we took the tour and saw the Book of Kells. People raved about it, but I was, in all honesty, less than impressed. It was poorly-lit, because light might damage it, and their choice for the displayed illumination left something to be desired.

I liked the gift shop better, truth be told, and purchased a pen with a real shamrock in a little heart dangling off of it, and a Book of Kells magnet for my fridge. The picture there was prettier than the one on display in the actual book.

Then we headed west on Dame Street, towards Christ Church Cathedral. He showed me the Olympia Theatre, which had a pretty stained-glass awning, though I wasn't quite sure what its significance was, and we didn't go in.

"I'm just saying, if the guy wanted to seriously help out people, he wouldn't have an offshore bank account for the specific purpose of keeping his money away from the Irish government, and wouldn't be trying to get others to spend what little money they have, when he's got millions," I said. I couldn't remember how the topic of Bono had come up, but it had been somewhere around a brief side jaunt to St. Andrew Street and the old church now converted to a tourist center.

Milo nodded. "No argument from me. Irish economy's sufferin', an' he's throwin' his efforts at Africa. Not that it isn't admirable an' a good thing t'do," he added, "but how about a little help at home, aye?"

Our next stop was Dublin Castle. My very first Irish castle! There were lamps in the lobby that were taller than Milo; since he made me feel miniscule, I enjoyed seeing him dwarfed by something. And it was nice to get my mind off murder for a while, though I was still bothered, at the back of my brain. I got a full history of the Irish revolution and some interesting tidbits of information on my own ancestors, to boot.

The coolest part of the castle was touring the excavated remains of the original Viking castle underground. Apparently, they'd found it after one of the current castle walls had started collapsing, and when they'd gone in to shore up the foundation, they'd found a big hole filled with dirt instead of an actual foundation. The River Poddle, which ran alongside the Liffey but underground these days, had washed away the dirt and exposed what was left of the first castle.

Across from the castle and two blocks from Christ Church Cathedral, still on Dame Street, we noticed a very small shop selling heraldic items. Milo pulled me inside.

"Let's find yer name," my boyfriend said.

"I'm not particularly attached to it," I protested, then had to smile at the shop clerk. "Uh, hi."

"How can I help ya today?" that one asked. His accent bore a resemblance to Eithne's. I wondered if he was from Galway, too. He glanced at Milo, who stood quite a few inches taller. But then, Milo was taller than most people here. "Look up your name for ya?"

"Oh, I know mine," Milo said cheerfully. "Hennessy, from *O'hAonghusa*."

"What about you?" the clerk asked me.

I sighed. "Reynolds."

He set to looking it up. I had to admit, the shop was neat, if cramped. It wasn't Milo's fault that it played havoc with both my clairvoyance and my claustrophobia.

"Here we are," the clerk said. "Reynolds. German, English, also Irish. Where are ya from?"

"America," I responded. "But my ancestors are from all over."

"Any Irish?"

"Yeah, both sides. A little distant on my mom's side. I'm not sure about my dad's." There were times I wished I knew more about his side of the family. They'd made no effort to keep in contact after Dad had left, and what I knew came from Mom.

He gestured to the computer. "Well, here we are. Reynolds, from *mac Raghnaill*."

He told me about the sept the name came from. It was interesting, but not really something I was fired up about. Milo, on the other hand, had other ideas. He dangled a keychain with "Reynolds" on it in front of me.

"We'll take this, an' the print out."

The clerk introduced himself as John as he hit the "print" button. I attempted to protest Milo's buying me the stuff, but both guys ignored me.

"Fine," I said. "But I'm paying for the cathedral."

Milo just snorted.

***

The cathedral was stunning. As much as I'm leery of places full of spirits, I'm a huge sucker for old architecture. Christ Church Cathedral had both not in spades, but dumptruck-fulls. It was also surprised to find that Milo was right about the cathedral: it was peaceful here, and most of all in the crypt.

"There's a café down here?" I asked him in a hushed voice. "That's kind of morbid."

"And a gift shop," he said cheerfully. "C'mon,

let's have lunch."

So we did. Weirdly, it was the most relaxing place I'd been to in Ireland.

"I've been thinking about what your dad asked me to do," I said. "And I don't know how. I had a little bit of an advantage when poking around Rob's death because Adam talked to me, but the Gardai have no reason to talk to me anymore, since I already told them I only met Ciara the once."

He nodded. "I been thinkin' about that, too. I'm not happy he asked ya t'do this, but I think he's right, you're s'posed to. She appeared t'you for a reason, aye?"

Unhappily, I nodded. I poked at my "traditional Irish stew" with my spoon. "Remember last year, when you got mad at me for doing what your dad wants me to do?"

Milo frowned at his sandwich. "I still don't like it. But if you're meant to, how can I argue?"

I reached across the table and laid my hand over his. "Then help me. I won't do it alone and you can make sure I'm safe."

"Okay," he said. "Can't think of a way t'get outta it, so . . . Okay."

***

Since we had more time in the afternoon, Milo and I went to tour the other big cathedral in town, Saint Patrick's. The windows were much more impressive here, with several depicting Celtic knots. It was also Jonathan Swift's burial place, as he'd been deacon of the cathedral for years.

We walked back up to the River Liffey. I found some of the fanciful bridges that crossed it charming, though others were just utilitarian. There were dozens of old, highly-decorative buildings, most with no signs to indicate what their original purpose had been. Milo told me that the majority of buildings in the area were businesses on the ground floor and flats on the others, to maximize living space for the city's million-plus inhabitants. Still, the place was smaller than Provo, something I found mind-boggling.

I found the comic store that Mags had begged me to visit, and I purchased a plushy Dalek keychain for her. When squeezed, it uttered the infamous "Exterminate!" After some debate, I got myself one, as well. Hers was yellow, mine red.

Milo took my hand as we made our way back to the garage where he'd parked. It was late enough that the usual revelers were out in droves, partying how I imagined Mardi Gras would be, minus the bare breasts.

"Okay, scratch that," I said aloud as a nearby woman, cackling with drunken glee, lifted her top, flashed a group of guys, and ran off into the dark.

"Huh?" Milo was busy looking down at me, expression puzzled.

"Did you seriously not see that?" I demanded.

"See what?"

"Never mind."

***

Milo gave his father a call when we got back to the house as informed him that I would be taking the case, as it were, but he was responsible for expenses incurred and any difficulties the two of us ran into along the way. It was kind of fun to see Milo taking a stand against Lugh and his arrogance.

I e-mailed Maegan and let her know what we'd seen that day. I didn't want to discuss Ciara yet, so I left that bit out. Then I got settled in and wrote up a summary of everything we knew so far about Ciara and her death. It sadly wasn't much, and I didn't have a whole lot to go on. There were a million and a half people living in Dublin, and that didn't include all the tourists. Finding a killer in Provo, Utah, with a population of a little over a hundred-thousand, was a whole lot easier than what I was facing, especially without police assistance.

I stared at the screen for several long minutes, dismayed by the task before me. Finally, I told myself to put it away for the night, closed the laptop, and went to bed.

CHAPTER TEN

Muriel had asked if I felt comfortable running her shop for a few days, just if I wanted to, since she knew I had experience. Since it gave us a decent headquarters in Dublin proper to investigate the unfortunate fate of Ciara Murphy, I decided we'd start there and see what happened. Thus, Milo and I went to the shop on Tuesday morning.

I really liked Muriel's store. If I could, I'd totally redecorate the Broom Closet to be lighter and cheerier, just like this little building. That reminded me that I hadn't talked to Mags in a while, so I picked up Milo's cell off the counter.

"I'm gonna call home and check in with Maegan," I told Milo.

He barely looked up from a map he was pouring over, marking with red pen whatever locations he was finding important. I didn't know at the moment if it was relevant to Ciara, or if it was stuff he wanted to take me to see. I decided I didn't care.

Mags picked up on the fourth ring. "Hello?" she asked breathlessly.

"Greetings from Ireland!" I said.

"Peyton!" Maegan nearly yelled it. "Omigosh, how is it over there?"

"Exactly how I described it in my e-mail last night," I laughed. "It's great. I wish you could see it. You'd love it just as much as I do."

"How was the wedding?"

We chatted about the festivities for a bit. Maegan's been my best friend since we were fifteen, and there are times it feels like we're sisters. Since we're both only children, and we've both gone through losing our mothers, sometimes we really are as close as siblings. I missed her a lot right then and wished I had her perspective on things.

"Muriel's gorgeous. I both love and hate her," I informed her. "And my dress is awesome. I'm bringing it back with me; you'll have to see it."

Then I had to ruin it and tell her that one of the bridesmaids had died.

"What?" she gasped. "That's horrible!"

"And . . . it's business as usual for me," I concluded. "Ghost's haunting me, I have to do something about it, and I hope by any deity that's out there that I can do it before Muriel gets back. Milo already called her and told her the news; she wanted to come back, but Quinn pointed out there was nothing she could do and it was best for them to stay in France and let the Gardai handle it."

"I'm not thrilled with the idea of you looking into it, Peyt," Mags said. "But you gotta do what you gotta do. Just be careful, okay? I don't want a repeat of last time."

Yeah. Me, either.

I said good-bye to Maegan and hung up. Milo motioned me over to where he stood with the map.

He spread the map out before me and gestured to the red markings he'd made. "Here's what I've done so far. This is us, at the shop. Here's where they found Ciara. This right here is where ya last saw her. I dunno what other pubs you girls went to, but this is where Darcy lives, an' where Rose and Nell live."

"And where did Ciara live?" I inquired.

He poked a red X. "Here. Really not far from that last pub."

"Also not far from here," I put in. "We could start there, I guess, since it's closest. I wonder if we could get into the building? Even if I can't get into the apartment, I could see . . . Well, I don't know what I could see, but sometimes I can pick up things from living spaces."

Milo nodded. "We can give it a try."

***

We weren't able to get into Ciara's apartment building. It was one with a keyed-entry foyer and neither of us had that key. She also hadn't had a roommate we could talk to. I wasn't sure about talking to her parents, just to get into the place and snoop around. I'd done that before, back in Utah, but it had been unavoidable when I'd run into the victim's mother while trying to pick up psychic impressions.

I got nothing useful from the little alley outside the building here. Ciara hadn't lived in the building long enough to leave an impression at the entryway, and nothing traumatic had happened at this site for a good while.

The only spiritual remnant I came across there was a little girl who'd died of cholera just before the potato famine; I didn't have the time to help her move on, and she didn't seem upset by her circumstances. Reluctantly, Milo and I left her there and backtracked to the last bar from the pub crawl Friday night.

"This is where we all parted ways," I said, as we stood on the sidewalk outside. "Rose and Nell went south, I'm assuming to their flat, Ciara went south-west, and Muriel and I headed back to the house. Darcy went partway with us, to the garage. Ciara seemed fine, if tipsy, but she didn't have far to go. Her apartment's only three blocks away."

Milo stood with hands in pockets, shoulders hunched against a slight drizzle as he looked around. In the mid-afternoon, the place had a different look than it had at night, but it was still packed with people getting drunk. I didn't understand the culture, maybe never would. Milo's expression said he didn't understand it, either.

"I'm not getting anything," I confessed. "Too many people around muddying the waters."

"Could be she picked up her killer at another pub," he suggested. "Or at work. We'll need ta check there."

"Yeah."

We abandoned that pub and wended our way towards the next-to-last place, retracing the party's steps as best I could remember them. We passed by a man taking donations for the families of alcoholics. I hesitated, then dropped a handful of change into his can.

"You know," I said conversationally, once we were out of earshot, "if there weren't, what, six hundred pubs in the city? They probably wouldn't have such a problem with alcoholics."

Milo wrinkled his nose. "Aye. They're an institution, though. Back when Catholicism was banned, they'd meet in the pubs an' hold church there."

"Really? That's kind of cool. And odd."

"No one questioned people getting' drunk of an evening," he informed me. "But it was illegal t'meet for Mass."

"Huh."

I got nothing at the next stop, either. Milo arched a brow at me at the third establishment on the list, a place called Whiskey Fish Grill. It was a stupid name that made no sense to me, but I guess the owner liked it.

"How many o' these pubs didja girls hit?" he asked.

I had to think. "Um. Five? I dunno why they thought it was such a blast, I was largely bored out of my mind."

"Aye, I can't see ya pub-crawlin', even if I know ya were on one."

"As I told Muriel, I was the sober sheep-herder."

He laughed, drawing a bit of attention from sleepy-eyed regulars and a few bright-eyed tourists.

As we had at the previous two places, I took a picture of Ciara and Muriel to the bartender, Milo close behind.

"Excuse me," I said. "Were you working Friday night . . .?"

The guy behind the bar was slender and not very tall, but had just enough muscle that one didn't want to mess with him. He studied me with hazel eyes, not even glancing at Milo.

"Name's Declan. Aye, I was. You're here about that girl on the telly, the murdered one. I remember you from t'other evenin'. One o' the hen party, was it?"

I nodded and held up the picture. "This is the girl. I know you've probably talked to the police, but I was hoping you might remember something more?"

Unlike the previous bartenders, who hadn't been on duty that night and didn't much care, Declan looked at the picture and frowned.

"She was the one kept orderin' the girly drinks an' flirtin' wi' Tom o'er there."

He inclined his head towards a young man leaning against the bar, apparently the bouncer, who was cute but in my mind, nothing special. His most outstanding feature was his body-building arms, which would probably make an inebriated customer think twice about messing with *him*.

I'd seen Milo shirtless, though, and knew this Tom guy was just for show.

"Mind if we talk to him?" I asked Declan.

"Knock yerself out."

Milo sat at the bar and ordered a beer while I made my way over to Tom. The kid was younger than me, and flashed a smile when I approached.

"Hiya," he said. "Somethin' I can do for ya?"

He was projecting images of what he'd like to do so powerfully that I didn't even need to touch him for my clairvoyance to pick it up. I suppressed a shudder and held up the picture.

"Declan says you were a big hit with my friend here the other night," I began.

"Yeah?" he replied warily. The lascivious light left his eyes. "What's it to ya?"

"Are you so out of it on 'roids that you're that mentally deficient?" I asked him. "She was murdered, idiot, and I'm trying to find out who and why."

His eyes went wide, and he tossed down the cloth he'd been idly wiping the already-dry bar with.

Tom got all of three steps before Milo closed the distance, snagged him by the collar of his shirt, and hauled him backwards.

"Not a good idea," my boyfriend said. "Makes ya look guilty as hell, runnin'. We ain't even the Gardai. We're just concerned friends, aye?"

Declan leaned on the bar, looking amused. "I should hire *you* t'keep the unruly in line."

"Appreciate the offer, but I'm livin' in America wi' my girl, here." Milo gave him a brief grin. "You got a place we can talk t'Tommy here, in private?"

I ignored Milo's comment about living with me--generally easier that way--and followed Milo and our reluctant guest to one of the back rooms.

"I didn't kill 'er," Tom said, as soon as Milo pushed him down in one of the room's two chairs. "I just had a bit o' fun with her."

"Define 'fun'," I said. I narrowed my eyes, hoping for menacing.

I'm not sure if it worked, but Tom was already about ready to pee his pants from Milo's hauling him around, so he spilled his guts instantly.

"We shagged," he said on a sigh. "When Dec wasn't lookin', we had a quickie inna back room. Er. This one, act'lly. She gave me 'er number, wanted me t'meet her later, after she'd seen you gels off, but I didn't call her. She was fun, but I got a bird at home. So I tore it up."

If he had, his number would have been in her records and the police would have spoken to him already. At least, that was my guess. I didn't think anyone had thought to question Tom before we did.

I knew she'd left this pub alive, with me, so I highly doubted Tom had had anything to do with her murder, but I still needed to verify his words.

"In here?" I asked him.

He nodded.

The only flat surface was the table; it looked like this room was usually used for poker games or something. I grimaced, bracing myself, and placed my hands on the scarred wooden surface.

It took a second, mostly because of my qualms, but the image rose, engulfing me.

***

They do it quickly, so her friends don't notice she's gone. Or his boss. This is a good job, and while it gets him a lot of bolloxed scrubbers, he doesn't wanna mess it up. He glances at his watch as he finishes buttoning his pants.

She giggles while she fixes the short dress she's wearing, the fuchsia beads of her necklace dangling between her very fine knockers. The cup's crooked, and he fixes it for her.

She hiccups, then grabs a scrap of paper and a pen someone left behind during the last round the night before, and scribbles her name and number on it. "Call me, yeah? I gotta ditch these others, but we can meet up at my place."

He watches her saunter out, only slightly wobbly on her heels, and then looks at the paper in his hand. The name is barely legible, the number partially smeared. He thinks of his girlfriend, waiting back home with their stupid little mutt dog, and sighs.

Tom tears the paper into tiny shreds and goes back out to work. He's not gonna call her. He never calls them.

***

Milo had a hand on my shoulder when I came out of it. I gave myself a shake and reached up to give his hand a squeeze.

"He's telling the truth," I sighed. "He didn't see her again after we left here."

Tom was looking at me with wide eyes. "Well, aye, but how'd I convince ya so sudden-like?"

I shook my head and walked past him, pausing to pat the top of his bleached hair. "If you really want to make it up to your girlfriend, buy Gordie a new chew toy and that dog bed you keep telling her you'll save up for. And stop sleeping with the patrons, it's skeezy."

He was as white as his polo shirt when we left. I waved at Declan and we stepped out into the rain.

"The look on his face," Milo said with a snicker. "I take it Gordie's their dog?"

"Terrier-something mix, maybe Pomeranian," I said. "I got a brief picture of it because he thought about the dog while Ciara was leaving. The kid's a moron. And what's a 'scrubber'?"

Milo coughed mid-laugh and his face went pink. "Ahh. I think the American term is 'slut'?"

"Oh. That's what I thought."

***

Since we'd struck out with the pubs, and Ciara's abduction had apparently not occurred at home, that left us with two options: check her workplace to see if she'd disappeared the night of the rehearsal, and check out where her body was found. Since I didn't want to deal with the crime scene just yet, I voted for work, and Milo, fortunately, agreed with me.

As expected, the Gardai had already been in to interview Ciara's coworkers. I let Milo lead this time, since I was somewhat worn out from my reading back at Whiskey Fish. What we discovered was that no, Ciara hadn't made it to work the night of the rehearsal. No one knew anything beyond that. And one of the waitresses hit on Milo.

"Helpful," I said sarcastically as we left the restaurant.

"Actually, it was," Milo countered. "We know she disappeared before the rehearsal. Now, if she'd be so kind as t'show up an' talk to us-"

He paused, waiting. The ghost didn't appear. "Ah, well," he sighed. "Worth tryin'. Wanna visit the museum, since we're in the area, then hit Merrion Square?"

"I suppose. We've run out of other options, except for abandoning this all momentarily and driving out to see Kilkenny, like you promised."

He chuckled. "Tomorrow, we'll go see Kilkenny Castle. Promise."

***

The museum was the National Museum, specifically the section on Archaeology. They had a fantastic exhibit on gold and weapons and things. I saw the Tara Brooch, which actually had nothing to do with the Hill of Tara, though it was very lovely.

"Ah," Milo said, grabbing my arm as I made to enter the exhibit on kingship and sacrifice. "Ya don't wanna do that, I'm thinkin'."

"Why not?" I asked.

"Bog people."

I arched a brow. "Bog people? Seriously? Cool!"

He sighed and followed me into the room. There were big round walled things in the middle of the room. I wandered into one, saw the skin of half a person lying on a table, and immediately backed out.

"Nope," I said. "Nope, nope, nope, nope."

"Toldja," my boyfriend muttered.

I gave a full-body shudder. "Icky! I didn't mind the skeleton of the lady over by the gold exhibit, but eek, bog bodies are nasty."

Milo laughed at me. "I *said* you don't wanna go in here. Let's bail, get dinner and then visit Merrion Square."

I was all-too-eager to flee the bog people, with their orange, leathery skin and lack of complete limbs.

"There are still peat bogs all over," Milo told me as we hunted down dinner. "Most aren't deep enough t'get buried in, since there's the peat industry. But every once in a while, ya find somethin' like those fellas."

We had dinner at a place purporting to serve authentic American food. I didn't see what was so exotic about it: a hamburger is pretty much a hamburger anywhere. Then we walked over to Merrion Square, east of Kildare Street and south of Trinity College.

"You know," I said as we approached, "we never did find where Rob was murdered or where the rest of him is."

Milo grunted. He wasn't overly fond of my

deceased ex, who sort of "lived" with me. Mostly, Rob hung around because I was the only one who could see and talk to him. And I had his TV.

"So Ciara appeared to us Sunday night, about, what, six hours before the cops were called about her burning body. I'm guessing she died shortly before we saw her. I don't think this is the primary."

Ciara had been stuffed into a wicker chest, one sized for blanket storage at the end of the bed, and then doused with an accelerant. The news reports said petrol; I said gasoline. Ultimately, same thing. Yellow crime scene tape still marked one corner of the square off as a crime scene, but it was falling off and tattered.

"I think they've downgraded this from an active scene," I commented to Milo.

"Looks like," was his only reply.

I sighed and trudged across the grass to the oblong charred area. I could see what Lugh had meant by a ritual: the energy was still a whisper in the back of my mind, and the burn marks, to the trained eye, indicated a circle had been laid around the makeshift casket.

"I don't think this was a real ritual," Milo said after a moment. "Or at least, not started by someone who knew what they were doin'."

He crouched and pointed to the circle. "This is wobbly. Nowhere near a perfect circle. It's rained since, but this white residue looks like salt crust t'me. Druids are known for the wicker burnings, at least accordin' to legend and the Romans, but we don't lay a physical circle like this."

I was fascinated. Milo rarely spoke about

actual Druid stuff, mostly referring to rites that Wiccans had appropriated over the years. "I didn't know that," I said.

He stood and brushed off his hands. "There's no point in a circle like this," he informed me. "Sure, henges are in a circle, but those are dedicated sites, set up t'be used time an' again an' need alignment. Or needed. They're off a bit now. Anyway, we don't do anythin' that would require a protective circle, 'cause we don't do summoning of the kind ya'd need t'lay one for."

"Like demons and stuff, Key of Solomon rituals," I said.

He nodded. "I think this was arranged t'confuse the authorities. Not us."

I scanned the scene, imagining how it would have been two days previous. "No," I said slowly. "The actual ritual was the murder itself. This was an elaborate body dump. Ciara's not here, and I'm not feeling anything of her that has been here. All I'm getting is . . . Okay, this might sound crazy, but it feels like the earth is offended by this."

Milo looped an arm around my shoulders, a faint smile on his handsome features. "I said there was more to ya than just seein' ghosts."

"So I'm right?"

"Aye. It's right pissed off. We done here?"

I hesitated, but had to concede defeat. "Yeah, we're done."

CHAPTER ELEVEN

I hadn't been intending to go in to Muriel's shop that morning, but Milo answered a call as we were eating breakfast, and said we needed to meet someone in town.

An older woman met us at the store. She had shoulder-length reddish brown hair, and a few crows' feet around her eyes. I pegged her for a normally cheerful person, but she wasn't smiling today.

"You're Muriel's brother," she said to Milo. "I can tell right off. Thanks for meetin' with me, but I've a question to ask you."

I unlocked the shop and we all stepped inside. Milo guided the woman to the office while I locked the door so that we didn't get walk-ins off the street. Milo let me sit at the desk, while he perched on the corner of it.

"I should probably explain who I am," the woman said, once we were settled. "I'm Moira O'Flynn. Muriel and your mother hired me to be her florist for the wedding. I got the flowers ready, as requested, but I had a call Saturday night that my father's in hospital down in Cork. My assistant was supposed to be bringing the flowers by for the ceremony and all."

I nodded. "The flowers were delivered, yes. The driver was a little late, said they got lost."

She didn't look surprised. "Well, that helps me a bit. Y'see, I just got back in to town this mornin', and I found my shop open and a right mess. Van's gone, paperwork for the wedding delivery isn't finished. And the arches Ms. Hennessy rented from us weren't returned afterwards. It looks like my assistant never came back, so I'm trying to figure out . . ."

"At what point they stopped comin' to work," Milo finished.

"Yes."

"Have you tried calling?" I leaned my elbows on the desk, frowning. This wasn't good. Two people connected with the wedding disappearing?

Moira nodded and sighed. "And no answer. I guess the next step is contacting the Gardai."

Milo gave her a grim look. "That's what I'd do, aye."

We escorted her to the door. As she stepped out to the sidewalk, I said, "For what it's worth, your assistant seemed fine when he left."

Her eyes widened. "'He'?" she repeated. "My assistant's name is Jennifer, and she's quite female."

***

Without even having to discuss it, Milo and I immediately escorted Moira to her shop. He explained to her what had happened to Ciara. I knew we were thinking the same thing: what if the mystery delivery man was the same who'd killed Ciara?

Moira was right, the store was pretty much a mess. The remains of assembly for the floral pieces were everywhere, and half-done paperwork covered the desk in the office, filled out in an appropriately flowery woman's hand.

"It looks as if she was intending to clean up when she got back," Moira remarked. Her gaze fell on the blinking light of her answering machine. "Oh, the messages. If you'll excuse me a moment . . .?"

I stepped out of the office to let her listen to approximately eight increasingly irate customers berate her company, her services, and even herself. It was obvious that the assistant had failed on more than one delivery.

"I don't like this," Milo muttered. He picked up a stray leaf and rubbed it between his fingers. "Ciara goes missin' Friday, this Jennifer on Saturday or Sunday mornin'. What do y's'pose chances are they're *not* connected?"

"About, oh, four and a half million to one?"

We all pretended we hadn't heard the shouting on the answering machine and Moira placed a call to the Garda. The same detective that I'd spoken to about Ciara arrived about half an hour later, with two uniformed officers.

Det. Ins. Byrne did a double-take when he saw us. "Didn't I just speak t'ya on Monday?"

"Aye," Milo said. "An' this lady here's me sister's florist. Makes one think, don't it?"

We went outside to talk to him, and explained how we'd come into contact with Moira. He was less than amused at the thought that Ciara's murder and Jennifer's disappearance were connected. He also didn't like that we seemed to be sticking our noses into his business, so Milo just explained that given the circumstances, he'd felt it best to stick with Ms. O'Flynn in case anyone unsavory stopped by.

"And interviewin' Tom the bouncer at Whiskey Fish?" Byrne inquired mildly.

I shrugged. "I was the only sober one that night, by the time we got there. I wanted to make sure I was remembering her talking to him correctly."

The man eyed me suspiciously. "He was sayin' something about an American woman, which could only be you, Ms. Reynolds, and his terrier. You have any idea what that was about?"

"Nope."

After about an hour, we were allowed to leave. Milo and I walked the four or five blocks back to Muriel's shop in silence.

"Well. That was fun," I said as Milo let us in. "What's next, the priest going missing?"

He snorted. "Hope not. Tell ya what. Let's take that drive out to Kilkenny now."

I sighed. "Sounds good to me."

***

Milo had been promising to take me down to Kilkenny Castle and to show me the Brownshill Dolmen; since we were at a standstill with Ciara's murder, there wasn't much we could do in Dublin. And I wanted to get my mind off it, and the missing florist.

The landscape was gorgeous. I snapped at least a hundred pictures just in the first hour of the drive. It was amazing to pass by little farms with the ruins of centuries-old churches in the middle of their pastures.

"This place is incredible," I told Milo as he drove. "If I could live anywhere besides Utah, it would totally be Ireland."

"That so?"

"Yeah. It's so peaceful and . . . green."

He made a left by a hardware store and drove down a winding road until we reached a small parking lot and a sign that said "Brownshill Dolmen". It surprised me a little that there were no other cars in the lot. For a supposedly famous landmark, it was completely deserted.

I looked around as I got out of the car. The field seemed to have recently been harvested. As we walked down a very long path, I asked, "So what's usually planted here?"

"I dunno. I'm assumin' potatoes."

Mike had been correct; the dolmen was a very, very large rock. The structure towered over Milo, and made me feel very small. From the nearby plaque, I learned that it was the only--so far located-- unexcavated dolmen in Ireland, and had the heaviest capstone of any dolmen in Europe. Given that the capstone was over a hundred and ten tons in weight, it was pretty obvious why it remained unexcavated.

Milo and I stood by the "door" of the portal tomb and studied the grass at our feet.

"So," I said. "There's dead people down there."

"Yep."

"Huh." I glanced up at him. "Seems this trip is pretty much about dead people and leprechauns."

"That's Ireland for ya," was his only comment.

After the obligatory photos, we got back in the car and continued to Kilkenny. It was a beautiful castle there, perched on a hill overlooking the city, but the interior wasn't very impressive, and they didn't allow photos. That was somewhat disappointing. More disappointing was lunch in the café there, in the former kitchen. I loved the décor and the ambience. The annoyingly aloof Danish waiter was a check in the cons column.

". . . Four Euro for a little sippy box of orange juice?" I said. "Seriously?"

"Tourist gouging," Milo commented. "I said we shouldn't eat here."

"But, castle kitchen!"

He snorted and shook his head.

We wandered around the city for a bit, and checked on the supply of jewelry Muriel had on sale at the artists' center across the street from the castle. I fell in love with the yarn used in a hideously

M. Roberg

expensive sweater, and vowed to locate some to take back with me.

"You know," Milo commented as we drove back towards Dublin, "I don't think I've ever toured Kilkenny Castle before."

"I liked the cathedrals in Dublin better, to be honest," I told him.

"Hmm."

He made a detour off the highway and wound through little roads, through the Wicklow mountains. I remarked as we drove that the mountains here were only foothills compared to the Rockies.

"Aye, but these are much older," he pointed out.

"Still. We live at a higher elevation than the tallest peak in Ireland."

The hills were green and yellow, the flowers of the gorse in full bloom. Milo pulled into a visitor's lot and parked. As we exited the car, he warned me, "Don't touch the gorse. It may look pretty, but the thorns are wicked bastards."

"Worse than roses?" I inquired wryly.

He held up his fingers, an inch apart.

"Oh. Yeah, that's worse. So where are we?"

"Glendalough," he informed me. "Valley of the two lakes, but I don't think you're interested in those. I'm showin' ya the monastic city."

I lifted my eyebrows. "Monastic city?"

He just grinned and gestured for me to follow him.

Milo hadn't been kidding. The monastery of Glendalough was now in ruins, but it sprawled over acres. There was even a huge watch tower. But what was really mind-boggling was the cemetery. The graveyard went on and on, some headstones as recent as the early 2000s, and some so old that they were just lumps of time-worn rock, listing or fallen over.

"Holy crap," I breathed.

He gestured to the walls-only remnants of a thousand-year-old cathedral. "Cathedral of St. Kevin. He's also got a church in his name in Dublin, both without their roofs."

There were tourists here, in droves, but what really took my breath away were the spirits that wandered through the graves: an elderly lady in her Sunday best sat on a low rock, speaking to a monk in coarse brown robes. Two more monks walked with a child in eighteenth-century clothing.

"Wow. I've never seen anything like this," I told Milo.

"Thought you'd appreciate it."

"I do. But, uh, can we get out of here before they realize I can see them and they start talking to me?"

That apparently hadn't occurred to him. ". . . Right. It's supper time, anyway. Let's go have a bite at the hotel over there."

I didn't question why there was a hotel in the middle of nowhere, at a site full of dead people, but as Milo had said, that's Ireland for you.

Dessert was chocolate chip muffins, baked in tall cups. They were the best thing I could recall eating. Full to bursting with chocolate chunks, they were made with real butter, and fresh out of the oven, the chocolate melting all over my fingers.

Milo watched with amusement as I devoured my muffin, then passed me the remains of his. "I take it you like them."

"I've decided I'm moving to Ireland for the baked goods," I told him. "I've never had anything like this before. It's even better than that chocolate lava thing at Chili's."

He shook his head and rolled his eyes. I was too blissed out on chocolate to care.

It was early evening, but not yet dark, when we left Glendalough. We had about thirty miles to go back to Dublin. Milo jokingly asked if I wanted to drive. I just glared and got in the passenger side of the car.

"Hey, why don't we swing through and see if the florist's stuff is still there?"

Milo tipped his head, considering. "I'm sure the Gardai have been there already. We've been gone all day."

"Just humor me," I cajoled. "Please?"

He relented, and we detoured towards Glencullen. According to the map I carried with me everywhere, it was faster to return to Dublin that way anyway, rather than drive back to the M9. We were just on the outskirts of Enniskerry, driving at a really annoying five miles an hour due to sheep, when I spotted the truck.

"Look! Look! It's the florist's truck! We have to stop!"

Surprised, Milo pulled over. I bailed out of the car and trudged into the pasture. I could see why the sheep were in the road: whoever had driven the truck into the fenced-off pasture hadn't secured the gate very well, and it hung open for all the little wooly quadrupeds to escape.

If we hadn't been going so slowly, I don't know that I would have noticed the truck. It was hidden behind a shed. The only reason I recognized it was because I'd seen it at the hotel the afternoon of the wedding, when Milo and I had gone to set up his guitar stuff. I got a chill when I remembered running into the man I'd thought was the florist. Had I actually had contact with Ciara's killer?

"I'm callin' the Gardai," Milo said, pulling out his cell phone as we approached.

"Good idea." I knew not to touch anything, and was fairly careful where I stepped, and not just for tracks. There was a lot of sheep poop in the pasture.

Even before I got to the truck, I could smell it. I clapped a hand over my mouth and fought the urge to gag.

"I think," I said, my voice muffled by my hand, "we just found Jennifer."

CHAPTER TWELVE

We sat and waited in the car for two guards to come in their ugly, official vehicle and check that yes, indeed, there was a dead body there, all right. Then they called in Det. Ins. Byrne, who didn't look surprised this time, just resigned.

"Any reason I shouldn't suspect the two o'ya?" he asked amiably, when he approached where we waited. "You always seem to be wrong place, wrong time."

"Just bad luck," Milo sighed. "We wouldn'ta found her if not for the damned sheep."

Said sheep were still milling about, and someone had been fetched to locate their owner, while the Garda technical bureau--their equivalent of

CSI--lamented the sheep crap all over their evidence.

"So why are you in this area?" Byrne asked.

"We went out to Kilkenny and Glendalough," I told him. "I told Milo that as long as we were out here, we should drive by the hotel, jog our memories and all. We didn't get there, obviously."

The detective looked over towards the truck. "Yes, I see that."

"I was drivin', and suddenly, sheep," Milo put in. "Had ta stop, obviously."

A ewe wandered our way, looked at us with beady black eyes, and blatted, "Meeheheheh!"

"I'll be takin' your statement later," Byrne told it, and I snorted.

"How'd you find the vehicle?" he continued.

Milo gestured at me. "I'm worryin' about sheep, an' Peyton yells 'The truck!' Recognized it from Saturday. Since we knew it an' the florist girl are missin', we called it in an' waited. That's about it."

Byrne nodded. He seemed friendly enough, but I knew he was still suspicious. I would have been, too, in his position. "Wait here," he said, and went to speak with the crime scene techs.

"He's not going to tell us what they find in there," I said to Milo. "Even if there are prints. We're just bystanders and, technically speaking, persons of interest. And he isn't Adam."

Adam Wallace, a detective with the Provo Police Department, had become something of a friend since the whole thing the previous fall. Milo knew I'd gone on one solitary date with the guy, before we were official, but hadn't made an issue of it. I appreciated that.

We got back in the car, and waited some more. It was full-dark before Det. Ins. Byrne came back over and said, "Seems t'be our missing girl, all right. Medical examiner will have to determine when she died, but it appears t'be sometime last weekend."

"Probably Saturday," I said. "'Cause she wasn't the one who delivered the flowers to the wedding or the reception. I'll bet she came in Saturday morning to get the flowers from the shop, loaded them in the truck, and he grabbed her then. That way he doesn't have her taking up space in the truck overnight and making the flowers smell weird, even with the refrigeration on."

Byrne lifted a single, auburn brow at me. I was willing to bet that the reason his hair was so short was because it was those tight, kinky curls guys get embarrassed over.

". . . I watch too much *CSI*," I admitted.

He refrained from comment. "You're free t'go," he said. "But don't leave. I don't care t'make this an international incident an' get Interpol to bring ya back if I need to talk with you again."

"Not going anywhere," Milo assured him. "C'mon, *cailín*. Let's get back."

***

I was starting to think of Muriel's house as home away from home. The place was still unknown, and I kept forgetting where the glasses were, but it felt safe.

We ate left-over wedding cake--not the stuff in

the freezer for the bride and groom, just the other stuff--and then I sprawled on the sofa and he sat on the floor beside me, with a dram of whiskey in hand.

"So why are you special and have three given names, and Muriel's only got two?" I asked.

Milo grunted softly. After a moment, he looked up, apparently realizing I wasn't going to accept a random noise for an answer. "Because, before Da left, he told Mam that if she had a boy, to name him Manannán. He didn't give instructions for a girl."

"How very archaic and patriarchal of him," I said. "So why that name?"

"Manannán raised him."

"Oh. Wait. Didn't Manannán's wife have an affair with Cú Chulainn, your half-brother?"

Milo nodded.

I shook my head. "Your family is so messed up."

"What about your father?" he asked.

I shrugged. Apparently, today was a day for discussing absentee parents. "They made a deal: she got to name the girls, he got to name the boys. Unfortunately for him, after Mom named me what she wanted, there wasn't a boy."

Milo arched a dark brow. "What happened?"

I didn't even wonder anymore how he knew there was more to the story. "When I was three, almost four, Mom had a miscarriage, and she started hemorrhaging. The only way to stop the bleeding was a hysterectomy. That was kind of . . . the beginning of the end for their marriage. Dad couldn't get over his need for a male heir. And then his daughter started talking to dead people, and he took off."

We were both quiet for a long time, lost in thought.

Finally, Milo said, "Really, I'm fine with all girls. A boy would be nice, but they don't have to be male to use weapons."

I laughed, trying to ignore the funny little flutter in my stomach. "Spoken like a man."

I ran my hand over his hair; he caught it and kissed my palm before lacing his fingers through mine. "Let's go sight-seeing in the morning. I've been in Ireland a good five days and haven't seen much of it."

"Sounds like a plan," he said. He took a sip of his whiskey. "Just wish this was goin' the way I'd hoped."

"Things never go exactly according to plan," I told him. "Unfortunately, that's life."

Milo nodded. "Aye."

I squirmed over and kissed the top of his head. "I like your mom."

"She likes you," he replied. "Which is good for me."

Laughing, I sat up and moved to join him on the floor. "Your dad, on the other hand, freaks me out."

His smile was wry. "You're not the only one, *cailín*."

***

Toasted

I decided that, previous attempts to open the shop having failed, I just wasn't going to bother running Muriel's shop while she was gone. But we'd gone through most of the perishable food in the refrigerator, and were all out of milk.

After breakfast on Thursday, I put my shoes on, shoved a five Euro note in my pocket, and told Milo I was running to the Spar to pick up some milk and a loaf of bread.

"Back in a few," I told him as I pulled the door shut.

The little convenience stores were like mini-grocers. They dotted the area the way Starbucks did back in the US. There was one not far from the house, so I headed that way, humming a little under my breath.

I'd looked into Ciara's death as much as I could; I'd got the impression she didn't have much to do with it, and had been randomly chosen. It seemed that Muriel had more of a connection than Ciara did. After all, if Ciara had been the target, why kill the florist and take her job at the wedding? It made no sense.

I wasn't, however, about to tell my suspicions to Milo. Not that my boyfriend was stupid; he'd likely put two and two together when Jennifer had gone missing.

So lost in my musings was I that I walked right past the store. A block on, I blinked, looked around, and cursed myself for an idiot. Turning back around, I trudged back the way I'd come.

A man stepped out of one of the alleys between the buildings right as I got to it. We bumped

into each other, and he caught my shoulders to keep
me from falling.

"Sorry," he exclaimed.

"No, no, my fault. I should watch where I'm-"

I looked up, into eyes black as night, and-

CHAPTER THIRTEEN

My first thought upon consciousness was that I was really cold. My second was that I hurt everywhere. The arm I'd broken last fall ached terribly. I could tell immediately that, just like then, I was bound hand and foot.

Crap.

I was in a small stone room, or maybe a cavern. It wasn't very bright in here, and water dripped somewhere in the distance, a monotonous tapping that would soon drive me nuts.

I tried to remember what had happened, but for the life of me, it was a blank. The last thing I recalled was telling Milo I was running to the closest Spar for a jug of milk, and stepping outside the house. Then . . . nothing.

"Awake at last."

Something moved between me and the sole torch that lit my prison. I blinked up at the speaker. He was backlit, so it was difficult to make out his features. Dark hair, pale skin, dark eyes. A thin nose. He looked familiar, somehow.

"I've been waiting hours for you to wake. I forgot how long humans can sleep after being given that herb."

His voice was what did it. I realized belatedly, with no small amount of confusion, that I was looking at the Brendan guy from Muriel's wedding. He just looked really different. His face was deathly white, his eyes pitch black. His hair hung in greasy, dark clumps around his face, not the stylish shag he'd worn before.

He bent towards me and something dark shifted behind him. It was only when I focused on the shadow that it suddenly clicked. The dude had *wings*. They were not of flesh and bone, nor feathers, but big, ragged sweeps of shadow that sucked in the light.

I stared. "You have wings?" I asked stupidly.

He paused, hand outstretched, and flexed his shoulders. It was strange to watch the dark nothing wrap surround him as he brought one wing around himself.

"Courtesy of my father," he said proudly. Then he glowered. "The only thing I have left now, thanks to your boyfriend's sire."

"Huh?" I tried to remember any stories about fey with wings, but nothing came to mind. I knew the Fomori were often deformed, with horse heads and extra limbs and stuff, but . . .

"Lugh," he snapped. "Lugh the hero, who killed my father and destroyed my people."

Brendan stepped away for a moment and light from the torch flooded back. I wiggled around and managed to sit up, but it wasn't easy. Fortunately, my captor paid me little attention.

"So, I decided, when I woke from my imprisonment, to have revenge. But I can't touch Lugh. Not yet. I need to harvest power." Brendan glanced at me. "And I can torment Lugh in the process."

I leaned my head back against the wall. A clot of dirt fell on my scalp, but that wasn't a real big concern at present. "Who was your father?" I asked.

Brendan's black eyes narrowed at me. It was easier to see him from across the room than up close. "Surely you've heard of Balor?"

"Oh, yeah. Sure have." Crap, crap, crap. And abruptly, it clicked in my memory where I'd seen him before: the previous fall, when Lugh had sent, via Eithne, a gold torque to his son, I'd touched it and had a vision that had knocked me on my butt. In it, I'd seen a pale, black-winged man with pitch-dark eyes emerging from the shadows, and he'd said one word. "*Díoltas*." Revenge.

"I need my revenge. But I can't face Lugh yet," he repeated. "So I'll take from him what he took from me. Family."

Lugh's father, Cian, was dead. Brigit's kids had killed him, which was one of the reasons they didn't like each other. The only vulnerable flesh and blood Lugh had were his children.

Cold fear for Milo surged through me. Instantly, I knew what my role was.

Bait.

***

I had no sense of time in the underground chamber. Brendan brought me a bottle of water and a vacuum-packed bologna sandwich. He untied one hand so that I could eat, but looped the rope around the bindings at my ankles. I hate bologna, but I was so hungry then that I wolfed it down.

My kidnapper laughed from where he reclined against the far wall. "Don't you humans have myths about taking food from the fey?"

I flipped him off and sipped at the water. He laughed again.

The next time he came back, I said, "I have to pee."

Brendan clearly hadn't factored that into his kidnapping. Finally, he untied my legs, led my outside, fastened my hands in front of me, and tied my "lead" to a nearby tree.

"I'll be back in two minutes. If you're not done . . ."

He didn't finish the sentence, but he didn't need to. I did my business, casting my gaze wildly around for anything that might help. All I saw was pitch-darkness in any direction. Completely unhelpful, aside from letting me know that we weren't near civilization.

The third time he visited, he informed me that

he'd given "my lover" a token: some of my hair, shorn while I'd been unconscious, and left with a place name only.

"And what place is that?" I asked wearily, sensing he really, really wanted me to.

"*An Bogach*," he said proudly.

I stared at him.

He looked disappointed at my lack of reaction. "Buggagh Bog, human. Even if ya get out of those ropes, good luck escaping. You're in the middle of a rather large peat bog."

***

I slept. I dreamed, and the dreams were frightening. I stood on a battlefield, where tall, strong men and women battled with monsters out of legend and horror films. All around me, warriors from both sides drew blood, wounded, fell under their enemies' weapons.

A roar rent the air, and a thing appeared, through the armies. It was huge, easily eight feet tall, with three eyes in its face: two in the normal place, one in the middle of the forehead. The third was closed, but when he opened it, a beam of hot light speared out and cut a swath of death and destruction before him.

Balor, of the Evil Eye, king of the Fomorians.

I woke with a jerk, startled, but it was still dark in the cold, stone room. Brendan had taken the lamp with him this time. I curled up, hunched over against the dirt mound, and squeezed my eyes shut, willing sleep to come back.

It did, eventually, and the dream continued.

I watched as countless *Tuatha* died, throwing themselves against the giant. He struck down a tall, shining warrior with flowing red hair, and the grief that rolled through the *Tuatha* hurt as if I, too, had been gutted.

And then, a young, blonde man stepped out of the throng, with a slingshot in his hand. With a start, I recognized Lugh, but as he had been thousands of years ago.

"Grandfather!" he shouted, in a voice not quite as deep as it would eventually become.

Balor turned, his ordinary eyes widening. "No!" he shouted.

Lugh picked up a stone, armed his slingshot, and let the missle fly. It struck Balor right smack in his deadly third eye with enough force to shove the orb out the back of his head, its killer light burning a hole in the ground where it landed.

Since the rock had gone through Balor's brain, it killed him instantly. The giant wavered, swayed, and fell, the crash shaking the ground.

Stunned silence fell on the battlefield, and then a cheer went up from the *Tuatha*. Enraged by Nuada's death and encouraged by Lugh's win, they were spurred on to defeat the enemy. As they charge with renewed fervour, I caught a flash of green eyes that filled my mind, just an instant before I woke.

Now you know, a whisper said, in the back of my mind, but I didn't know the voice.

Know what? I wondered. I already knew Lugh killed Balor. What was I supposed to gain from that?

Feeling grumpy, sore, and immensely frightened, I struggled to go back to sleep a second time. I wanted to be rested for when Brendan came back.

***

"Psst."

I jerked out of sleep at the harsh whisper. I'd finally managed to get back to sleep, and apparently, Brendan had come and gone again, though he'd ever-so-kindly left an electric lantern hanging where the torch had been.

Ciara's ghost crouched in front of me. The eyeless sockets, dripping with blood, were still unnerving. Fortunately, the dim light made them hard to see.

"You've gotta hurry," she said. "The dirt you're leanin' on? About a hand-width in from where you're sittin, there's a knife. I can feel it. There's somethin' special about it, yeah? Hurry."

"What did he do to you?" I asked her. I straightened and turned my hands to the dirt pile, scrabbling frantically with half-numb fingers at the hard-packed soil. "Why do you look . . . like that?"

She shrugged. "Somethin' that he did t'me when he killed me. He took my eyes, said they were the windows, an' the doors. I think he meant, like, the eyes are the windows t'the soul? 'Cept my soul's right here. So what'd he take?"

"I dunno, but I'm gonna ask someone who might know." My hands hurt, and I'd broken at least two nails. I hadn't found the knife yet.

M. Roberg

Suddenly, she straightened. "Hurry! He's coming."

She disappeared. I doubled my efforts, and finally, the tip of one finger snagged something cold and metallic. I'd just freed it from its ancient prison when Brendan walked in.

It was dark, though, so he couldn't see what I'd been doing. I reclined over the hole.

"Still alive?" he asked me. "Good. No sign of your lover, or his murderous sire, yet."

"Go die in a fire," I told him.

He smirked and knelt before me, way too close for comfort. "I like your spirit. I'd been planning on taking it, but maybe I'll keep you. You have such . . . fire."

He trailed a hand down my cheek. I jerked back, shuddering.

"I did you a favor," he told me, as he sat back on his heels. "And ya don't even know it."

Brendan made a "tsk tsk" sound. "Someone locked away a bit o' your power, y'see, an' I let it out. I almost want to let you loose on the world an' see what happens. Mayhap I will . . . after I kill Milo."

"You hurt him and I'll cut your balls off," I growled. "With a dull, rusty spoon. And no anesthetic. And then rub lemon juice and salt on the wound."

He arched one raven brow. "You, lass, have quite the nasty imagination."

He stood and went to the door. "If he's not here by sundown, I'm afraid I'll have to kill you anyway."

Sundown. Okay. But what time was it *now*?

After he left, I sat back up and worked at getting the crusted dirt off the knife. Then I turned it on the ropes. Moisture ran down my hands; whether it was sweat or blood, I didn't know, but I was more interested in getting free than I was worried about cutting myself.

After what seemed like hours, the rope around my wrists slackened. Blood rushed into my fingertips and I gasped at the pain of it. My hands shook as I turned my attention to the bindings on my legs. What nails I hadn't broken off earlier snapped as I clawed at the damp, muddy rope. Finally, I grabbed the knife and sawed through one side.

Brendan walked in as I freed my right ankle.

"How did you- Stop!"

He grabbed at me and I ducked. His hand closed on my hair and he yanked me to my feet. Brendan tried to take the knife away and I twisted; he grabbed my left wrist, the one I'd broken six months before, and pressed hard, almost digging into my skin. I squealed in pain and tried to pull away.

I stabbed at him as we struggled, catching him in the upper thigh, almost in the groin. I'd been aiming for his abdomen, but he'd shaken me and I'd missed. Brendan screamed like a girl and let me go. Blood spurted from his thigh wound; I was betting I'd hit the femoral artery. Awesome.

My left foot was still fairly numb, my right filled with pins and needles. I hobbled away and he stumbled after me. Whirling, I lashed out with the blade and slashed him across the face. He screamed and fell back to the floor.

I bolted.

It was daylight now, the sun near the middle of the sky. That didn't tell me much, though; it could have been late morning or early afternoon. He was right; I was in the middle of a freaking peat bog, and I had no sense of direction. The angle of the sun told me nothing, and with my watch broken, I had no idea what time it was.

The knife tight in my hand, I ducked around behind the pile of rocks I'd emerged from. Honestly, who sticks a dolmen in the middle of a bog? Brendan wasn't immediately forthcoming, so I took off across the drier sections of bog.

I lost a shoe almost immediately, but the other stuck with me as I trudged through the muck, staving off horrifying visions of falling into some deep well of peat and being found centuries later, looking like those people at the museum. As I walked, I catalogued my possessions: a knife that looked to be made out of bronze, crusted in dirt and blood; one shoe; a 5 Euro note in my pocket. No wallet, no passport, no ID of any kind. Also, no idea where I was.

What looked like a chunk of old wall rose in front of me. I took a breather and sat down on it. My arm was burning and throbbing. A blister the size of the pad of Brendan's thumb had weltered up on the inside of my wrist, flaming red and painful. I used the knife to tear a strip of my tee off and I wrapped it around my wrist, mostly to keep dirt out if the thing happened to pop.

I couldn't stop for long, though. I hopped over the wall and found myself on slightly sounder footing. Ten more steps and I was on solid ground and running as fast as I could. Green grass appeared, and then gorse bushes.

Eventually, I had to stop running. I fell to my knees, tearing my jeans and jarring my hands. I panted for desperate breath and looked up at the sky.

The sun was farther from the zenith, which meant I had only hours until Brendan's sundown edict. That was, if he could catch me.

Yeah, right, idiot, my Inner Voice said. *He's got wings.*

"Not helping!" I responded. My voice was hoarse. I needed water, but had no idea where to find some.

Some time later, I came across another low wall, this one separating two very verdant fields. The wall was probably older than the Magna Carta. All I cared was that my wrist was screaming at me and I was getting so thirsty, I was dizzy.

I peeked at the blister and made a face, suppressing my gag reflex by swallowing hard. It had filled with yellow-green pus and streaks of blood, which did *not* bode well for my continued health if I didn't find my fellow humans soon.

I looked at the dagger. It was small, less than seven inches from end to end, the leaf-shaped blade the bulk of it. A rounded, somewhat Roman hilt connected the blade with the ridged handle. The pommel was round and shaped like a puffed disc. Holding it was a bit awkward, but its weight was comforting.

I wiped what I could of the dirt and blood off on my already-stained jeans, and stood. On the far side of the left field, ran a dirt road, now mostly overgrown. I trudged across the calf-high grass and stood in the road, trying to decide which direction to take.

A fox skittered by me, then stopped and dug a burr out of the fur on its haunch.

"Hi," I said to it.

It looked up and blinked brown eyes at me.

"I'm lost," I told the fox.

It hissed and ran away, into the grass.

I yelled after it, "Same to you!"

Ciara popped into view in front of me and I shrieked, almost throwing the knife. She was even more gruesome in broad daylight.

"Hurry. He's coming."

"Brendan?"

She nodded.

"Crap."

I picked a direction and started running.

CHAPTER FOURTEEN

I've never been much of a runner, mostly due to short legs, bad knees, and large breasts. You try running a relay with big sacks of fat on your chest and tell me how you do.

Ciara kept up with me. I don't know why.

I had to stop, and I bent over, panting, hands braced on my legs. I squinted at the ghost. "Can you find Milo?" I asked her. "Tell him where I am?"

The empty eye sockets just regarded me, the ghost unnervingly silent.

Okay, then.

"Think," I said aloud to myself. "If Brendan was imprisoned in that tomb when his father was killed, and he was with Balor and his army when

Lugh offed Ol' Ugly . . . Balor died near . . . some lake in Sligo."

Problem was, County Sligo was across the island from Dublin.

If Brendan really had given a message to Milo, he and Lugh would be able to figure that out, too. I just had to hope I was headed towards Dublin, because to stay near the dolmen was suicide.

The sun dropped lower in the sky, almost to the horizon. I was beyond exhausted, so thirsty I didn't think I'd be able to talk if my life depended on it, and there were blisters on top of blisters on my feet. I'd been walking for hours, and somehow hadn't run into anyone. No farmers, no tourists. Zip, zilch, nada. My only company was a mute and creepy ghost.

The road eventually broadened and turned, exiting through gorse bushes to join with a gravel road. It wasn't fun pushing my way through the inch-long thorns, even if the yellow flowers were pretty. Milo had been right: roses had nothing on these things.

It started raining just before full dark. I turned my face to the sky and desperately gulped the little drops of water. Trudging along through the gloaming, soaking wet, I started singing to keep myself occupied.

"Please," I said aloud. "If anyone's listening, please let Milo find me."

Darkness fell.

I'd been stumbling along for about an hour in the pitch black, keeping time by singing the lyrics to "Phantom of The Opera", when I saw headlights in the distance. I was so surprised, I almost tripped over my own feet, and I cut off in the middle of "Wishing You Were Somehow Here Again".

My muscles hurt everywhere, and my feet were two lumps of pure agony, but I hurried as fast as I could on the wet and somewhat muddy gravel, waving my arms frantically, hoping that the driver would see me and stop.

The vehicle slid to a stop not ten feet from me, the headlights blinding after so much darkness. I couldn't see what it was, but I guessed a truck from the height. I shielded my eyes from the glare with an arm.

The passenger door opened and someone got out. I couldn't see a thing.

"Please," I said, choking words out with my ragged voice. "Please help. I'm really, really lost, and I'm hurt-"

"Peyton?"

Milo's voice came to me out of the darkness, and then suddenly he was crushing me tight against him, hauling me clear off the ground and kissing my face. I threw my arms around him and broke down sobbing, unable to hold it back any longer.

He slid an arm under my legs and carried me to what I now saw was an SUV. Lugh was behind the wheel, and he reached into the back to fetch a thick blanket. He spread it out on the seat and Milo set me on it, then somehow came up with another one and wrapped it around me.

"How did you find me?" I whispered.

"Hush, *a stór*," he murmured. "Drink this."

It was a flask of whiskey, but at that moment, I

seriously didn't care. I gulped, choked, nearly spat it back out, but in the end, I managed two swallows. It stopped the shaking, at least.

"You drink this stuff on purpose?" I gasped out.

Milo climbed into the back with me and Lugh put the truck in gear. He explained that they'd been hunting for me for two days, in and around Dublin, even had the Gardai out and looking for me. Then they'd received Brendan's message. They'd driven all night towards Sligo, only stopping for gas, and since dawn had been going in circles looking for me.

"There's a dolmen in the middle of the bog," I told him. "It's hard to get in and out of."

"How in Danu's name didja get away?" my boyfriend asked.

I nodded at the ghost, who'd taken up sitting in the front passenger seat. "Ciara, and this." I held up the knife, but I'd been holding it so long, I couldn't let it go.

Milo carefully opened my fingers and, with barely a glance at the ancient weapon that he tossed on the floor of the back seat, massaged the feeling back into my hand. He spoke in a low voice, entirely in Irish, as he did. Between my exhaustion and the alcohol, I fell asleep within minutes, with my head on his shoulder.

***

I woke when Lugh parked in the lot of a hotel in Sligo. We probably could have found one closer to where they'd found me, but Lugh wanted comfort and security, and neither Milo nor I were about to argue. His father booked us a suite, with two rooms; Milo and I had one, and Lugh had the other. Milo didn't want to let me out of his sight, and I didn't want to let him.

When we got to the room, Lugh went to order room service, saying as he retrieved the menu that in the morning, he'd see to replacing my ruined things as this was, he felt, his fault. I didn't say it, but I agreed. It *was* his fault.

I stripped out of the muddy, torn clothes I'd been wearing for the last three days and dropped them on the floor. The only thing really salvageable, and it was a big maybe on that, was my bra. But I'd been in it for so long, I wanted to burn it with the rest of the heap. Sighing, I shoved it all into the corner and, with many aches and pains, took a long, hot bath.

Washing tangled hair only makes it worse, really, but I couldn't brush it with the mud and who knew what else in it. Once it was clean, I dried off with one of the hotel's big, fluffy towels and wrapped up in one of their equally fluffy robes. When Lugh picked a place, he picked posh. There was even a comb in the toiletry set in the bathroom. I preferred a brush, but I'd take what I could get.

I went out to the bedroom and sat on the king-sized bed, comb in hand, and began the attack on the three days' of snarls infesting my hair. It wasn't until Milo came over and took the comb out of my shaky hand that I realized I was crying again. Feeling a bit like an invalid child, I sat and let him patiently work the tangles out.

Room service brought up the food Lugh had ordered. Milo brought our trays into our room so I could eat in privacy, as I *was* only clad in a bathrobe. It was thick, hearty lamb stew, with potatoes and carrots, and hot soda bread on the side. I forced myself to eat slowly, so I wouldn't make myself sick. It was good to get something other than water and bologna.

Once I felt vaguely human again, I let Milo bandage my various injuries. I bundled up in the quilt before Lugh came in to take care of the mess on my wrist.

"Nasty bit o' business, there," the fey muttered. He produced a pocket knife and some matches, sterilized the blade, and sliced the blister open.

That part wasn't too bad. I couldn't feel the skin anymore. It was when he pressed on the sides to force the infection out that I had to bite down on a rolled-up hand towel and do my best not to scream. I *did* scream when he poured hydrogen peroxide over it, but it was muffled by the terrycloth.

Milo dabbed sweat off my brow. "S'okay, *cailín*. We're gonna bandage it up now. Almost over."

He put me to bed with several pain relievers and some tea. I suspect it was laced with whiskey, but didn't care. I slept mostly in a fetal position, with Milo curled protectively around me.

***

I was running through the bog again, but I knew I'd escaped. How was I back? Had I hallucinated being rescued, or was this a dream?

"You can't run from me," Brendan's voice said, somewhere behind me. "I will find you."

I heard the flap of wings, felt hot, fetid breath on the back of my neck. I ran faster, but the bog was sucking at my feet. I stumbled and fell, found myself sinking into the peat. It pulled me down, down, into its cold, wet clutches, and I heard Brendan laugh as the slime closed over my head.

***

I woke on a choked scream, flailing to get free of the mire. Hands grabbed at me and I fought wildly, until Milo's voice reached me through the panic.

"Hush, *cailín*," he said. "Hush now. You're safe. It's only a dream, *a stór*."

I forced myself to relax, rolling over to curl into him. I was under the sheet, he was over it, which didn't make snuggling easy but kept my modesty relatively intact.

"I have a new worst fear," I whispered.

He smoothed a hand over my slightly-damp hair. It always took forever to dry. "What's that?"

"Turning into a bog person."

Milo didn't smile, though I could tell he was tempted. "I think that should be any sane person's nightmare. Imagine bein' stared at all day, lyin' there in a museum, naked and in bits."

I worked a hand out from under the covers and

smacked his harm. "Jerk."

"Aye, but you're smilin'." He kissed my forehead. "Go back to sleep, Peyton. You're safe. I'm not goin' anywhere."

I burrowed closer, buried my face against the curve of his neck, and did as ordered.

CHAPTER FIFTEEN

When the shops opened in the morning, Lugh sent Milo out to get me the new clothes he'd promised. I wrote a list of the things I needed, and in what sizes, and my boyfriend went off with his father's credit card. I was too exhausted, emotionally and physically, to be embarrassed at the thought of Milo buying me underwear. All things considered, though, better him than Lugh.

"How is your arm?" Lugh asked me, as I poked listlessly at the eggs and sausage room service had delivered.

I had the robe tied as securely as I could manage, and was all-too-aware of being half-naked in a room with my boyfriend's father. Grateful for some sort of distraction, I pulled up the sleeve of the robe and looked at the bandage. Something had seeped through the gauze, so I took it off and we both made faces at the renewed pus filling the wound.

"I don't like the look of this," Lugh admitted. "Cleaning it should have removed the infection, and for it to fill this quickly . . ."

"Yeah, I'm not too thrilled, either."

He studied me for a long moment. "I don't know what medicines would help, because I don't know what he did to you."

I had even less of a clue than the god did, which didn't make me feel any better about the infected thing on my forearm.

The door opened and Milo came in, carrying several shopping bags. He frowned when he saw my arm was no better.

"We could cauterize it," Lugh suggested.

"Ugh. It's already been burned, thanks. I'd like to put that option off unless nothing else works."

Milo shook his head and went to get the peroxide. I didn't scream this time, but it was no less pleasant than before.

Once it was re-bandaged, I dressed in the clothes Milo had brought back. A black tee, nothing special. A sweater of pale blue cashmere, lightweight and soft, very appreciated because I couldn't really seem to get warm. The jeans were dark blue, fortunately without the "trendy" rips and tears currently in fashion.

I had to smile when I saw the shoes. They were pale blue ballet flats of a soft suede, with grey-and-blue plaid on the toes and black patent bows. He had to have chosen them just to cheer me up, because they weren't the most practical, and hadn't he been questioning the practicality of my shoes just days ago?

The bra and panties were brow-raising. They matched, and consisted largely of very pretty black lace with nude-coloured backing in the important areas. They were some brand called Chantelle, and gave me a fascinating glimpse into Milo's tastes in lingerie. I had to wonder if he'd picked it out all by himself, or if he'd had assistance.

When I emerged into the lounge area from the bedroom, dressed in my new duds and feeling a lot better, Milo handed me a white paper bakery bag.

"I also bought ya this," he told me.

I snatched it and peered in, eyes rounding at the sight of a positively enormous slab of chocolate cake wedged into a plastic take-away box.

I looked up at him. "I love you."

He laughed.

I was only able to eat about half of it, and I probably shouldn't have had that much. I packed the rest of it back up for the trip back to Dublin. My old clothes I crammed into one of the shopping bags, and I was going to burn them as soon as I could.

***

I sat in the back-seat of Lugh's SUV—I hadn't known they had these over here, but apparently when you're a rich god, you can get hold of one—as we made the trip back. Ironically, I found that if I'd gone left instead of right when I'd hit that dirt road, I would have reached the R284, one of the largest roads in the area. Instead, I'd managed to mostly walk in circles through the lower part of County Sligo, not far from the border with County Roscommon.

"But if ya'd gone that way," Milo pointed out, "he mighta found ya. He's more familiar wi' the area than you are."

He had a point, one I didn't want to think about.

It took a large portion of the morning to drive back to Dublin. I spent most of it curled up in Milo's arms in the back seat. I was incredibly grateful to Lugh for helping look for me, but I wasn't about to snuggle with him. I wanted to see more of the country, but I felt a little feverish and my arm ached, so I was more interested in escaping into sleep than watching more fields full of sheep go by.

Explaining my reappearance to the police was something I didn't want to do. Milo, however, pointed out that if we didn't tell them, it could start an international incident. So Lugh drove us to the heart of Dublin and I sat down with Det. Ins. Byrne.

I explained that I hadn't seen my attacker, and he'd driven me out into the wilds and dumped me off after taking my money. Lugh smoothly filled in that I'd found refuge with a farmer until I'd been able to call Milo.

They weren't happy with that, but had to, ultimately, take me at my word. There was no way I was going to send them after Brendan.

Brigit met us at Lugh's flat, an incredible posh place at the top of an old building in south Dublin, near Trinity College. She was very sleek, with shiny red hair and a spotless wrap dress in teal green. She was almost more intimidating than Lugh. I thought I'd rather deal with Erin and Bonnie than with Brigit.

"I've been looking through our records," she said, and placed a very old book on the long, wooden table in Lugh's dining room. She cast an emotionless glance at our host, then flipped the book open.

"At the battle of *Magh Tuireadh*, when you killed Balor, apparently one of his . . . generals was his half-human son, Brendan, born to one of his concubines and not his wife, your grandmother. This makes Brendan your uncle, Lugh, though he's quite a bit younger. He was twenty-two at the time of the battle, and Daghda imprisoned him in a dolmen nearby."

I nodded. "That's basically what he told me."

She looked to me, inclined her head, and went back to the book. "It also says here that, ah . . . Brendan was known as the Soul Taker."

Milo frowned and braced his elbows on the table. "What's a 'soul taker'?"

Lugh reached over and snagged the book, pulling it to him so he could scan the text himself. I was looking at the page upside down, and all I saw was faint brown gibberish, not even Latin.

"A 'soul taker'," the god said after a moment, "is someone who is able to take the . . . life force of a person and break the bond between the body and the soul. Once it's taken, the soul is left to wander and the body decays. There is no out-of-body experience, the soul cannot rejoin the body."

I shuddered. "I think I know how he does it."

Brigit and Lugh both looked very interested at

that.

"How?" the goddess asked.

"He cuts out their eyes, and then he . . . carves whatever he needs to in their chest." I didn't need to look at Ciara to confirm what I said, though she was nodding frantically at me. "And he adds that . . . life force to his own."

We all glanced at Ciara; she hadn't left my side since Sligo. Going to the bathroom was awkward with a ghost in the room, not to mention showering.

Lugh handed Brigit the knife I'd taken from the dolmen and used to injure Brendan. "Do you recognize this?" he asked her.

She gasped, looked sharply at me. "Where did you get this?"

I shrugged. "It was buried in the dolmen? Ciara told me it was there, I dug it out, and I used it to get free."

Brigit held up the bronze weapon. Lugh had apparently cleaned it. It still needed sharpening, but it was in near-perfect condition. That, and their reactions, told me that it was no ordinary thing.

"This blade," the goddess said, "belonged to Aífe."

"Who's Aífe?" I asked.

"She was a goddess who'd been turned into a swan and then killed," Lugh said. "Manannán turned her swan-skin into a magical bag."

"Ew."

Milo chuckled at my expression. Then he turned serious. "Brendan obviously had help in this," he said. "'Cause that wasn't him that delivered the flowers t'the church an' the hotel. So who's his friend?"

"The guy we're assuming killed Jennifer," I added. "Her death didn't match up with Ciara's."

"No, it did not," Lugh said, in his low voice. His blonde hair was loose today, falling in his face as he continued to peruse the book. Finally, he snapped it shut and sat back in his chair.

"Muriel and her new husband return tomorrow evening, yes?" he asked Milo, who nodded.

The blonde giant sighed and rubbed a hand over his chin. "Well, there's nothing else for it. Brigit? Did ya bring what I asked for?"

The redhead nodded and picked up a work bag that she'd set on the floor by her chair. I admired the bag: deep, shiny red alligator texture leather, big enough for a laptop computer. She retrieved something from its depths and handed it to Lugh, who turned to me.

He held out a gold necklace. I gingerly took it, but only felt comforting warmth from it.

"What is this?" I asked him. The pendant was a tree, branches and roots connecting in a ring of knotwork, in which were caught a stag and some sort of bird. On either side, nestled in the knotworks, two women tended the branches.

"It's to protect you," he told me. "From Brendan and anything like him. I can't say what he did to you, because I don't know. But this should shield him from being able to sense you. It may create a barrier between you an' the dead."

"Oh, really?" That was interesting.

"Your family all used to have one, but the

blood became diluted an' humans began t'not believe in us. You come from at least one line o' people given the task o' gathering lost spirits and guidin' them to Manannán." He studied my face for a reaction. I wasn't sure how to take the information, but it wasn't a huge shock. "It has been a long time since someone as strong as you has existed, an' has had need o' it."

I looped the delicate chain over my head. The tree was only about an inch big, and it fell to my cleavage. Instantly, I felt different. I could still see Ciara in all her bloody glory standing behind Lugh, but that nasty feeling I'd carried since I'd woken in Brendan's dolmen lifted. I breathed a sigh of relief.

"So, I know that my mom's family is one of the lines," I said. "What would the other be?"

"You're descended from *mac Raghnaill*, as well. Your last name, Reynolds," Lugh said.

I had to snicker at that. "Oh, Dad would *love* to know that."

Milo took my hand and studied the nasty, ragged scab where the blister had been. "How'd he do this?"

"He burned me while we were struggling, I guess," I responded. "He grabbed my arm, I stabbed him with the knife, I ran. It turned gross really fast, so I know he did something to me."

Brigit nodded. "It's part of a tracking spell," she said. "The Fomori used it to brand their slaves. Bres was also fond of using it on his concubines."

I didn't like the sound of that one bit. Frowning, I told them, "He said that he unlocked something in me? That someone had locked away part of my power and he let it out."

Milo's hand went to the back of my neck and lightly rubbed my shoulder. He didn't like where this was going any more than I did; the hand at my back was his showing silent support.

Lugh shrugged. "I dunno who, I dunno when, but if things have changed recently for ya . . ." He inclined his head towards Ciara. "Then I'd say, yes, that happened."

Lovely. "Do I expect to see more nasty stuff in the future, then?"

"Probably. I'd have t'ask Manannán, he's the expert on the dead."

Brigit checked her watch, then stood. "I hate t'break up the party, but I've another meeting in fifteen minutes at the museum."

"Which museum?" I asked.

"The National Museum," she said. "Specifically, archeology. I'm on the board."

Oh.

Brigit left. I picked up the knife I'd found. It was a weapon of the *Tuatha*. That was more than a little mind-blowing.

"I suppose you guys want to keep this," I said to Lugh.

He waved a hand. "Not especially. Other than being one of our weapons, it's not a particularly significant one."

A dog came into the room then. I use the term "dog" loosely. I suppose it might have been a wolfhound, but it was the size of a small pony, with a shaggy, reddish coat. The thing sidled up to Lugh and put its head in his lap.

"No way," Milo murmured, borrowing a very American term I tended to use a lot.

"What?" I eyed the dog cautiously.

"Is that . . ." He stopped and eyed his father. "Is that Failinis?"

Lugh nodded and patted the dog on the head. I was completely lost.

"It's a dog," I said dumbly.

"Not just any dog, *cailín*," my boyfriend said. "This is a special dog. Out of mythology."

He held his hand out, and Failinis padded over on massive feet to sniff his hand. The dog snuffled and then butted his huge head against Milo's palm, wanting pets.

I put my head down on the table and sighed. My feet and my arm hurt, my throat still hadn't totally recovered from going thirsty for so long, and now I was staring at a mythical dog.

Failinis left Milo and came over to me. He whined and nudged me with his nose, then looked at Lugh and barked once. Lugh looked up from the book, eyed me, and frowned.

"What?"

Milo, too, turned his attention to me. He pressed the back of his hand to my forehead. "You're burnin' up, Peyton. Ya feel alright?"

"Honestly, no, I feel like crap." I coughed and reached for my glass of water. "I just spent the better part of three days held captive by a psychopath, inside a tomb."

One corner of Milo's mouth turned up at that. "Aye, ya have a point. Why don't ya go take a nap over there, while Lugh an' I discuss what t'do?"

That sounded really good. I nodded and went over to the suede-upholstered sofa, which was mounded with plush pillows. I dragged one of the throws over my lower half, wondering who did Lugh's decorating. Probably Brigit. Those two had one heck of a complicated relationship.

Failinis followed me to the sofa and flopped down, putting his head on the cushions beside me. I'm not a fan of dogs, but I really missed my kitty in that moment. A hound out of legend would have to suffice.

CHAPTER SIXTEEN

I felt somewhat better when I woke, but I still had something of a nagging cough. The fever had gone down while I'd slept, and I didn't feel like I was dragging through water just to get by.

Milo and Lugh didn't seem as tense with each other, either. I could tell Milo wasn't going to be instantly fond of his sire, but he also didn't look inclined to punch him in the face. Improvements all around, then, save for the ever-present and still-dead Ciara.

Failinis licked my hand and nuzzled against my side before wandering off for kibble in the kitchen. I sat on the edge of the sofa, wondering at the bizarre turns my life had taken. And to think I'd complained about just being able to see ghosts. Ha!

Milo had procured a wrap bandage for my wrist, to disguise my injury. As I put it on, I eyed the dog. A lightbulb went off in my head then.

"Hey . . . That sword you got," I said to my boyfriend.

"Aye?"

"Um. Could it maybe be, er, how do you pronounce it? 'Fragarach'?" Privately, I thought it sounded like *Fraggle Rock*.

He blinked green eyes at me, then turned to look at his father. "Lugh, did you give me The Answerer for my birthday?" he asked.

Lugh didn't look up from whatever he was reading. "Took you long enough," he muttered. "You're of age, why shouldn't I give it to you? I gave it to Cú Chulainn, fat lot of good it did *that* idiot. And don't get me started on Conn. Don't do anything stupid, Milo, I haven't any other sons to give it to."

There wasn't much either of us could say in response to that.

We left Lugh's flat shortly after, returning to Muriel and Quinn's house. I hadn't checked in with Maegan like I'd promised I would, since I'd been, you know, tied up in the middle of nowhere, and I spent a little while speaking to her long-distance. I couldn't take too long to explain, but I assured her that I was alright and I'd explain everything when I got home.

"So. Now what?" I asked Milo, after I hung up.

"We still gotta find who killed Jennifer, an' kidnapped Ciara for Brendan," he said. Then he pointed at me. "But I'm not lettin' you outta me sight 'cept t'use the toilet."

I had no argument there. "I wish Ciara would talk, but she's almost useless."

Milo watched the ghost for a while, as she drifted through the living room. "I think he broke her," he said quietly. "Maybe she *can't* say much."

The ghost put her hands over her empty eye sockets and silently wept. I felt awful for her. She'd been a ditz and a floozy in life, but no one deserved what Brendan, and her mystery kidnapper, had done to her.

"Ciara?" I said gently. "Can you talk to me at all? I need to ask you some questions."

She stopped crying and wandered over. There was definitely something different about her than the other ghosts I'd encountered, appearance aside. Maybe Milo was right; whatever had happened to her had damaged her soul.

"I want to help," she whispered. She'd closed her eyes, or what was left of them.

"Was it Brendan who took you?"

Ciara thought for a moment, then shook her head. "No. A human. A man."

"Was it the same man who . . . put you in the park?"

She nodded. "I can't remember his face," she told me plaintively. "Can't remember-"

"It's alright. Don't make yourself upset," I said quickly. "You've made a lot of progress, but don't push yourself."

Okay, that was a really weird thing to say to a ghost.

I yawned, nearly pulling a muscle in my jaw when I did. "Ow," I muttered. "Okay, I need to go up to bed. I'm still *so* tired."

"Yeah, you go," Milo said. "I'll finish up down here an' come join ya."

Well, that was a nice thought. I didn't want to sleep alone, still. Just the idea of it sent a shiver down my spine as I headed for the stairs. Once in my room, I quickly changed into pajamas, re-bandaging my arm and feet in the process.

I felt bad for Ciara, but I couldn't sleep with her in the bedroom, staring at me. The only reason I'd been able to sleep before, when Milo and Lugh had rescued me, was because I'd been too tired not to.

"Um. Ciara?"

Her head lifted, but I couldn't say she *saw* me. It was still unnerving to look at those empty sockets, though they weren't as shocking as before.

"Is there somewhere you can . . . go?" I asked her gently. "I don't know what to do for you right now, and I feel . . . bad that I need to sleep and . . ."

"I understand. I dunno why I look this way." She pulled at her hair. "I don't understand any o'this."

Sighing, I sat on the bed and folded my legs under me. "I've been at this a while, but everybody's death experience is different. I wish I could wave some magic wand and tell you everything's going to be okay and you're going to move on to where you need to go, but I still don't know how this stuff works. I don't know why some people get stuck and others move right on. I don't know where they go when they do. And I don't know how to . . . fix you."

She nodded. "Milo's dad seems to have ideas."

"That's because he was raised by Manannán mac Lir, the sea god who's also in charge of ferrying spirits to their destination." I leaned my elbows on my knees, folding my hands under my chin. "I'm going to do what I can to help you. But it might take a while, and I don't know if I'll have to go back to the States and then come back here."

She meandered over to the window, one that overlooked the street. I wondered how much she could see, if at all, or if her appearance was just a manifestation of her trauma. Her hand went through the curtain, and she pulled it back, balled a fist. The tears that leaked down her cheeks were stained red. I felt even worse now, and didn't know how to ask her to vanish so I could sleep.

Milo appeared in the doorway, in a dark blue tee and grey sleep pants, barefooted. Ciara was oblivious. I held out my hand to him and he came over to sit on the bed.

"Has she said much?" he asked me in hushed undertones.

"More than before. I think talking to her is helping-" I yawned suddenly, with a force to nearly pull a muscle in my jaw. "-Helping bring her back. Sort of."

"You should sleep, *cailín*." Milo ran a finger down my cheek.

Abruptly, Ciara turned. "I should go," she said, and was suddenly gone. Poof, vanished.

I gaped. "Freaks me out when they do that," I muttered.

Toasted

"You were lookin' for a way to get rid of her," he pointed out. "I heard ya talkin'."

"True, but that doesn't make me feel any less weird or guilty about it."

I flopped down on the bed. After a moment, Milo stretched out beside me.

"You mind?" he asked.

"I don't want to be alone," I admitted. "When I was kidnapped last fall, I knew you'd come for me, because I sent Rob to find you. But this time . . . I knew you'd come, but I didn't know if you'd make it in time."

He wrapped his arms around me, pulling me close to rest his chin on the top of my head. "I would have kept lookin' forever," he whispered roughly. "An' when I get my hands on that-"

Milo broke off and pressed a hard kiss against my hair.

I tipped my face up and kissed him, my hands curling around the back of his neck. His dark curls were soft and silky against my skin. I tangled my fingers in them and rose on my knees, needing to be closer to him, wanting the security of his larger frame against mine.

His hands slid down to my hips. "Peyton," he murmured against my mouth. "Not a good idea t'be doin' that."

I shuddered out a breath. "I know," I whispered. "I just feel safer."

He twisted to lay me down on the mattress, and turned me in his arms to tuck my back against his chest. I had to admire his restraint, given I could tell just how much he wanted me, the evidence of his desire hard against my thigh. Normally, it would have embarrassed me, but right then, I didn't care.

"He won't get you," Milo said in my ear. "He'll hafta go through me, an' I'll kill 'im."

I fell asleep with that soothing promise echoing in my ear.

***

The buzz of the doorbell jerked me out of sleep while it was still dark. Milo caught my flailed arm with an amused snort and said, "Be right back, stay here."

I was back out before he'd even left the bed. Sometime later, I woke a second time, with a sense of unease. I wasn't sure how long it had been since Milo left, but he was still gone. I tossed the covers back, swung my legs out of bed, and stood.

Big mistake. The pains of my recent travails had really caught up with me, and moving hurt. My feet ached and my head swam. It was a good thing I'd brought pain killers with me in my carry-on, because they were prescription items in Ireland. I downed two ibuprofen and padded on protesting legs to the door.

Just as I opened it, Ciara appeared in the hallway. I barely managed to stifle a shriek.

"Darcy's here," she said, and vanished.

Oh, lovely.

The stairs in Muriel's house were old and creaky, so they had to hear me coming. Halfway down, I could see into the parlor, where Milo sat facing Darcy on the sofa. She was crying, and as I watched, she leaned over to kiss him.

I was going to *kill* the bleached-blonde bimbo.

"Milo?" I called, purposely loud. "Babe, you coming back to bed?"

To my utter amusement, Milo shoved Darcy away so hard she fell off the sofa onto her skinny butt. He looked offended and angry, which made me feel a little less homicidal.

I descended the rest of the stairs and entered the parlor. Darcy was just picking herself up off the floor, and her face was tear-streaked, eyes red.

"Uh," Milo said. "Darcy was . . ."

"I don't particularly care," said, "what her excuse is. You don't kiss someone else's guy, Darcy. Yeah, I saw that. And given the couple of days I've just had, if you don't vacate this house in the next minute, I will *make* you leave."

For once, she was wearing sneakers, probably the most surprising thing about her appearance. She towered over me and shoved her face in mine. She reeked of alcohol, and her sneer was extremely unattractive. I only felt a smidge of sympathy for her.

"He was *mine*," she said. "An' my friend is dead!"

Milo stood and moved to stand behind me, hands on my shoulders. "Darce, I toldja, I'm with Peyton now. An' even if she an' I weren't together, you an' I still wouldn't be gettin' back wit' each other."

He was angry with her; his accent had a tendency to thicken when he was emotional, and from his grip on my shoulders, I could tell he wasn't moved to paroxysms of joy by her words. I wasn't, either.

"Muriel will be back tonight," my boyfriend continued. "I heard ya out about Ciara, but my sister would be a better person t'talk to, aye?"

Darcy snatched her purse off the sofa and slung it over her shoulder. "Fine. I'll just drive meself home, then."

I hadn't considered how she'd gotten here. I couldn't in good conscience, as much as I disliked her, let her drive herself home in this condition.

"No," I said. "Milo will drive you, and I'll follow in Muriel's car. I don't like you, but I don't want you to smash into a building because you're drunk."

Ciara waited by the foot of the stairs. She followed me up when I went to get my shoes.

"I'm sorry she's bein' a tart," the ghost said. "If I could speak t'her . . ."

"I don't think Darcy would be particularly receptive right now to the whole dead-people routine," I told Ciara. "Maybe when she's sober. And Muriel's had a chance to talk to her."

"You'll . . . help me talk to Mure, right?"

I paused in shoving my feet into sneakers and looked at her. "Of course I will, Ciara."

"Thanks, Peyton," she whispered. "You're not the stuck-up American bitch Darcy said ya were."

She popped out again, leaving me wondering how, exactly, to take that particular comment.

***

Milo drove Darcy to the parking garage nearest her flat, and I waited there for him to return from walking her to her building. I was nervous about being in the car by myself, but with the doors locked, I figured that Brendan or his unknown human minion couldn't get to me without making a huge scene. Since we were in Temple Bar, even at half-past three in the morning, someone would notice.

I moved over to let Milo drive when he got back to the car. "Seriously, I can't believe you dated her."

He heaved a sigh and shook his head. "Like I said, I was young an' stupid. She's not always like this, *cailín*. Her friend *did* die, an' she's jealous that I'm in love wit' you."

Hearing him say it made me grin, even if briefly. "I know, which was why I didn't yank her hair out or something. She's got to be beside herself with worry over what happened to Ciara, and why, and we can't exactly tell her what we know. But I . . ."

I shook my head. "I'm petty enough, Milo, that I just don't care about her problems right now. I have had a very difficult week, and I'm still sort of in shock and wondering why I'm not gibbering in a corner after what Brendan did."

When we stopped at the light at O'Connell Street, just before crossing the Liffey, Milo reached over to thread his fingers through my hair.

"You're stronger than ya think, Peyton," he said. "An' bein' kidnapped isn't foreign to ya now."

"Thanks, I needed that reminder." I idly rubbed my arm, mentally tallying the injuries to it.

"We'll find Brendan," Milo said. "An' we'll deal with 'im."

Leaning my head back against the headrest, I watched the statue of Daniel O'Connell go by. Even at this hour, it was lit by floodlights at its base. I didn't want to think about Brendan, or Ciara, or anything horrible. I wanted to enjoy the vacation I'd originally been intending.

We drove past the Monument of Light, also known as the Spire of Dublin. It was a really, really tall sculpture, the world's tallest, and just glancing at it provoked my vertigo. I quickly turned my attention back to Milo.

"I don't know how to proceed," I told him. "I feel like that's all I say these days. I'm supposed to find who killed Ciara, and technically speaking, I've done that. But I don't feel like I've solved anything. Who kidnapped her? Who dumped her in the park and set her on fire? She says it wasn't Brendan. Brendan killed her, we know, but he had an accomplice. I just . . . I don't know how to find out who that is."

"Maybe," Milo said, "that part is for the Garda to figure out."

"Maybe," I agreed, but not whole-heartedly.

CHAPTER SEVENTEEN

When we got back to the house, we both collapsed into bed. Dealing with hysterical bimbos is exhausting, and I was already tired beyond belief.

I slept well into the afternoon, and woke feeling even more stiff and sore than before. I took a hot bath, which eased some of my muscle aches, and doubled up on socks to pad the sores and blisters from my trek through County Sligo. Milo was in the kitchen, doing whatever it was he was doing, when I limped down the stairs.

"Hungry?" he asked me when I appeared.

"Mostly thirsty, but I wouldn't say no to food."

He quirked a smile and fetched me a glass, instructing me to sit. When I'd drained the glass and some leftovers were heating in the microwave, he took a look at my wrist.

"I really don't like what that's doin'," he said, as we eyed the still-infected wound. "An' it pisses me off I don't know how t'treat it."

"Lugh said he doesn't know, either, and I got the impression that freaks him out." I pushed at the bubble of pus and watched with fascinated horror as some leaked out. "I'm just glad it doesn't seem to be spreading. Last thing I need is blood poisoning. At least the trip insurance would cover that. I think."

"Oh, my father would pay for it," Milo said darkly. "I'd make sure of it."

We cleaned it yet again and re-bandaged, and then I had a late lunch. Ciara appeared and flitted around the kitchen, but didn't seem to be in a mood to talk. I wasn't sure if it was us talking to her, or just time and distance, but she didn't seem quite as broken today as she had the night before.

"Didja want to come with when I pick up Muriel an' Quinn from the airport?" Milo asked me towards evening.

I'd been reading one of the guidebooks I'd brought with me, and bookmarked my place. "No way am I staying here by myself."

"That's what I thought. Their plane lands in about an hour, so get your shoes on."

It was a half-hour drive to the airport, mostly due to speed rather than distance. Milo drummed his fingers on the steering wheel for most of the way.

"Trying to decide what to tell Muriel about everything?" I asked him.

He shot me a look, obviously surprised. "Aye. How'd you know?"

"Because I'm wondering the same thing."

I liked the Dublin airport. It was big and airy, and while it was obviously modern, it still somehow had an element of that infamous Irish charm to it. That likely had more to do with the employees than the buildings themselves.

"Excuse me," I said to one particular older man, in a uniform declaring he worked there.

"Yes, miss?"

"Could you tell me, um, where I could find the ladies' room?"

He grinned. "Belfast."

Milo laughed. I socked him in the arm.

"Straight back through those doors, 'til ya hit the wall says 'Toilets'," the man said with a chuckle.

"Thanks." I glared at Milo and limped off to the restroom.

When I emerged, I found Milo sitting on a nearby bench, with a pair of slippers in his hands. They were a rather ugly, vivid pink, but they were hard-soled, and really, really fluffy inside. Styled like moccasins, they had pink sequins all over the outside.

"Thought these might be better on that foot," he said.

". . . Was that the only color they came in?" I asked.

"Nah. They also had 'em in orange, an' purple. And I know how ya feel 'bout those. So."

I took the pink slippers and said, "Thanks, Milo, you're the best."

I might have looked a little silly in my jeans, tee, and fuzzy, sparkly pink slippers, but they felt a *lot* better on my poor feet, and just that he'd thought of it made me happy. So I was in something of a relatively good mood when Muriel and Quinn appeared through security.

That didn't last very long, because Muriel burst into tears the instant she saw her brother, and threw herself into his arms. I looked at my fuzzy slippers and knew that while I was in pain from Brendan kidnapping me and everything else, hers was worse because she'd never see her friend again. I'd get over the sores.

"How was France?" I asked her husband.

"Oh, it was-" Quinn noticed the bandaging on my wrist. "What happened t'you?"

I shrugged. "Got kidnapped by a Fomorian and held in a tomb for three days, then he branded me like cattle and I had to run, barefoot, for miles through a peat bog."

He blinked, eyed my face somewhat desperately for a hint of a joke. ". . . You're not kiddin', are you?"

"I *so* wish I were."

He looked from me, to my wrist, then to the slippers. ". . . France was lovely."

"Glad to hear it."

***

We hadn't been back from the airport an hour when Lugh and Brigit arrived. Milo and I had just finished explaining the events of the last week to Muriel and her husband, minus Darcy's late-night visit, when the *Tuatha* rang the bell.

This time, Quinn went to answer the door. I couldn't hear specifics, but Lugh's voice was a deep rumble, pitched below Quinn's tenor. In a few moments, Lugh and Brigit followed Quinn into the kitchen.

Muriel immediately leapt to her feet. "I don't want him here!" she said angrily to her husband. Turning on her father, she pointed a finger at him. "This is your fault! Ciara's dead 'cause o' you, ya bastard, an' now you've gone an' dragged Peyton inta yer mess? How heartless *are* you?!"

The tall blonde man looked stunned at her outburst, more taken aback by the violence of it than that she was angry with him. Brigit smoothly inserted herself between them and took Muriel's outstretched hand in hers.

"None of us could have foreseen this," she told Muriel quietly. "Brendan's awakening, I mean. We lost all knowledge of him after the battle, the one in which his father was slain an' he was imprisoned. My father- my father should have told us what he'd done, but he didn't. We were reeling from Nuada's loss, and Brendan's imprisonment was lost in the shuffle."

"Your father."

"Yes. My father, Daghda. He spelled Brendan to sleep and sealed him in the dolmen until he could be dealt with, but when Nuada fell, he forgot about the boy. *We* forgot about the boy." Brigit looked to Lugh.

The king took up the tale. "We have been going through our records, and speaking to the kin we have . . . available. I only have a vague recollection of his presence at the battle, as I was occupied with defeating his father, Balor. I am truly sorry, daughter, that he has caused you pain. I cannot change that he did so, but I can take measures t'see that he does not hurt you again."

Muriel realized her hand was still in Brigit's and yanked it away, folding her arms, with a glare that encompassed them both. "An' how, exactly, do ya plan t'do that, *Father*? By usin' my brother's girlfriend as a bloodhound?"

Well, that wasn't very flattering, was it? Still, I knew what she meant, and I had the same reservations she did. I just knew I couldn't let those reservations get in the way.

"No," Lugh and Milo said in unison.

They blinked at each other, then Milo said, "No, Peyton's not gonna hunt Brendan down. Far as I'm concerned, she's done her part wi' Ciara, an' in a few days, we'll be goin' back to America. Surely the Garda got forensic evidence of *some* sort off that van. It could take a while, aye, but fingerprints, or DNA, or somethin'."

"What about the ghost?" Lugh asked. He turned those green eyes on me. "Has she said anything?"

I glanced at Ciara, who stood by the back door, empty eye sockets turned our way. "Only that it was a human who took her, and a human who dumped her at Merrion Square. Brendan is the one who killed her, but he doesn't seem to be venturing into the city proper."

"He grabbed you two blocks from here," Milo pointed out.

Toasted

Quinn spoke up for the first time since his erstwhile father-in-law's arrival. "But this area ain't Temple Bar, or the government district. I'm thinking his human friend is less noticeable, more average."

I didn't know if Brendan was still bothering with the glamor full-time, or if whatever he'd done to me let me see through it, but inconspicuous wasn't something I'd call the Fomorian prince. Tall, rail-thin, sickly-pale. And let's not forget the wings.

Frowning, I looked at Lugh. "Have either of *you* guys actually *seen* Brendan?"

The *Tuatha* exchanged looks, then shook their heads. I looked at Milo, and he did the same.

I sighed and rested my chin on my hand. "So, basically, I'm the only one who's seen the guy. Great."

Muriel turned her attention to me. "Be good to know what he looks like, wouldn't it?" she ventured. She was a little calmer now, but still visibly irritated.

"In case he comes after any of us?" Milo asked. "Aye. An' I'd like t'keep me eyes open for him, so I can kill 'im."

He looked at Lugh, and though neither spoke, I could tell they agreed on that.

Muriel stared at me for a few moments longer, then seemed to make a decision. "We could try sketchin' him, maybe. Like the artists who work with police on TV."

"I'm willing to try," I told her.

Brigit put her hand on Lugh's arm. "I think it would be best if we took our leave, let Muriel relax and concentrate."

Lugh obviously wanted to protest, but he took

one look at Brigit, glanced at Muriel, and nodded in silence. Without a word, he turned and left the house.

"A word, Peyton?" Brigit murmured, as I trailed after her to the door.

She drew me aside and pressed something into my hand. "I cannot heal the damage Brendan did. That magic only works for our kind, and it's been . . . a very long time since we've used it. But I may be able to help with the infection."

She'd given me a packet of herbs of some sort. I sniffed it.

"Take a third of the herbs, make a tincture, soak your bandages in it, and keep them wrapped as long as you can. You only need do it once a day for three days. I hope it helps." She gave my hand a squeeze.

I raised an eyebrow at her. "And how do you know, when the all-knowing Lugh can't do squat?"

Brigit sighed. She released my hand, turned her attention to the wide, simple gold cuff she wore on her right wrist. She always had some pretty bauble on, so I hadn't noticed anything special about today's.

The redhead removed the bracelet and turned her arm so I could see the thumbprint-sized scar on her arm, identical to mine. "As I said," she told me in a low voice, "Bres liked to use it on his concubines."

Before I could form a response to that revelation, she had the cuff back on and was pulling away towards the door. I just stared after her, unable to form any sort of response. She pulled the door shut behind her.

Toasted

Finally, I shook myself out of my daze and went to lock the door.

CHAPTER EIGHTEEN

"His cheeks are thinner, just a little bit, through here. And his chin is narrower. But yeah, that's good on the jawline." I tapped the sketch, indicating the places that needed changing. "And . . . Something's off about the eyes."

Muriel erased the lines she'd drawn, sketched them back in where I'd pointed. "What's off about the eyes?"

Chin in hand, I studied the drawing. It had been dark in the tomb, but I clearly remembered those eyes. They still followed me into sleep.

"No sclera," I said slowly. "Just . . . dark. All black, like demons on '*Supernatural*' or the black oil aliens on '*The X-Files*'."

"Ooh," Muriel said. "Aye, I remember those

aliens. Haven't watched this '*Supernatural*', though."

"It's Peyton's favorite," Milo put in from the parlor, where he and Quinn were watching a football match. "She really likes the car."

Muriel arched a raven brow at me. "Car?" she repeated.

"It's an awesome car." I grinned. "It's also bad form to drool over the hot stars in front of your boyfriend."

She laughed as she carefully filled in the eyes with the pencil. Somehow, she didn't make them look flat.

"I wish I could draw this well," I sighed.

"We all have our talents. I'm sure ya have some."

"Well . . . I can crochet," I offered. "I tried knitting, but all I manage is rectangles."

Squinting at the drawing, Muriel redid the chin so that it wasn't as broad. "My mam crochets. She makes Irish lace. Stocks her things in a few places around the country. The scarves in my shop? Those are hers."

"Oh, I noticed those. They're really pretty."

"I'll tell her ya said so." Muriel finished with the chin. "Anythin' else you need changed?"

I looked at the drawing carefully. Just the image of Brendan on paper was enough to send a chill down my spine. "No," I whispered. "That's him."

"Creepy," she commented, eyeing her own handiwork. "Can't say I find him attractive."

"Oh, one more thing," I said, suddenly remembering. "I slashed him across the face, his left cheek, about here. I don't know exactly how it would look, but I got him pretty good."

"Okay." Muriel added a mostly-horizontal scar, starting just under the outer corner of his left eye and crossing to his nose. "Like this?"

"I guess."

She wrinkled her nose. "Now he's just downright scary, ain't he?"

I shivered and my hand automatically went to the bandage on my wrist. "You have *no* idea," I told her fervently. "And I hope you never have to meet him."

"Mmm." Muriel put her pencils back in their case and zipped it closed. "So what's with you an' Milo sharin' a room now?"

My face instantly went red. "Um. Sharing?"

Her green eyes lit with amusement. "You think I wouldn't notice those enormous boats he calls shoes in by yer bed?"

Pressing both hands to my cheeks in an attempt to both hide and cool the flush, I mumbled, "It's not like that. He's been guarding me. We're not . . ."

"That's a pity," she said, and burst into a peal of laughter.

Quinn appeared in the doorway. "What's so funny in here, then?" he asked. He was obviously pleased to see a smile on his wife's face. It wasn't my place to ask, but I was betting she'd been pretty miserable on their honeymoon.

That reminded me: I still had some uncomfortable mediation to do with her and Ciara. But I didn't want to just yet. Selfish, maybe, but I still had injuries to recover from. Nothing was going to change the fact that Ciara was already dead. My taking some time to myself wouldn't alter or fix that.

Still, my conscience nagged at me.

"Just teasin' Peyton," Muriel told her husband. She stood and carried her art supplies back into her home office.

Quinn pulled up a chair. "Game's on half," he explained. "Everyone's talkin' 'bout Ciara an' how t'stop this Brendan guy, but what *I'm* wonderin' is, how are *you* farin'?"

I shrugged. "I'm having nightmares, obviously. And my arm's messed up."

"Morbid of me t'ask," he allowed, "but can I see it?"

Since I had to change the bandage anyway, I nodded. I pried up the tape and unstuck the gauze. I wasn't going to have any hair on my forearm after much more of this.

The wound was still raw, scabbed and pus-filled, the skin around it angry and hot. But it still hadn't spread. It wasn't a perfect oval imprint, and it slanted slightly across my wrist, imperfectly placed.

"What *is* it?" he asked.

"Thumbprint," I said. "He . . . apparently has the ability to burn a mark on people and use it as a . . . magical tracking device. This necklace I've got on is supposed to disrupt the . . . signal, for lack of a better word."

Muriel came back in, saw my wrist, and gagged. "Oh, that looks wretched," she said, stating the somewhat obvious. "Brendan did that to ya?"

"Yup." I got up and pulled the packet of herbs

out of my back pocket. "Brigit . . . gave me this, says if I boil a third of this, then soak my bandages in the tincture, and do it for three days, it'll stop the infection."

Muriel's nose wrinkled. "I wouldn't trust 'em far as I could throw 'em, but she probably knows what she's doin', 'least as far as this goes."

"That's what I figured."

Milo came in to see what was taking Quinn so long, and he, too, made a face at my wrist. "I'll help ya clean it," he offered.

"Thanks. Could you start these to boil? Brigit says it'll help. Just a third of the packet."

I handed him the herbs and went up the stairs to get the first aid stuff. As I reached the top of the stairs, Ciara appeared there, and I stepped right through her. We both gasped, and I stumbled to my knees on the wooden stairs, gripping the railing so I didn't fall backwards.

My vision swam. She reached for me, put her hand to my shoulder-

***

She's nude, now, and tied to some flat surface. A table? She can't tell. She hurts so much, after all his questions and the times he's hit her when she didn't answer fast enough.

He stands over her, eyes dark in the firelight. He smiles beatifically, like that Mona Lisa painting, and he raises a knife.

"I won't say this won't hurt," he tells her. "Because it will."

Then, with that same smile in place, he starts cutting. She screams, but no one can hear her. Endless screaming, until her throat is raw from it. Her skin is slick with blood, and he ignores her cries and whimpering, chanting in some language she doesn't know. Sounds a bit like Irish, but she never learned that.

Then he stops cutting, stops chanting. He moves to stand by her head, looking down at her with that infuriating smile.

"I'm afraid, my child, this part is the most unpleasant," he tells her, and the knife descends towards her face.

*** *

Hands lifted me off the floor, and I realized I was shrieking and blubbering, lying on the stairs, nearly in convulsions. Milo lifted me in his arms and carried me the rest of the way to the bedroom. It wasn't until he had me on the bed, in his lap, that I realized Muriel and Quinn were there, too.

"What's wrong?" Quinn asked. "What happened?"

"Vision," Milo said tersely. "C'mon, *cailín*, deep breaths. Let it go, *a stór*."

"I saw it, I saw it, I saw what he did, oh, God, I saw what he did to her. Make it stop, make it stop, make it stop!" Nausea welled and I scrambled out of his arms and off the bed, barely making it to the bathroom before I threw up.

Milo knelt beside me and wiped my face with a damp cloth. He pressed his hand to my forehead.

"You're burnin' up again. Back to bed, love."

"I don't want to see it again, please, don't make me," I whispered, hands reaching for him desperately. "If I close my eyes, I'll see it again."

"No, ya won't. I won't let ya."

His words didn't make any sense, really, but I clung to them as he carried me back into the bedroom. Muriel was still there, looking distraught, and Ciara hovered nearby.

"I'm sorry!" the ghost said. "I didn't know that would happen!"

"You need t'leave fer a bit," Milo said to her. She nodded frantically and vanished.

Muriel frowned. "Was she- Did you just talk t'Ciara?"

He nodded. "Apparently, she somehow triggered a vision fer Peyton."

Quinn came back, with a tumbler of golden liquid. He wordlessly handed it to Milo, who in turn handed it to me.

"Drink this," he said.

"This is whiskey."

"Aye. Drink it. It'll help."

"I don't drink!" I wailed.

"Ya t'ink I don' feckin' know dat?!" he thundered. "I'm tryina help ya, Peyton! Shut up an' drink da damn whiskey 'fore I make ya do it!"

Stunned into silence, I blinked. I looked from him to the glass. I *didn't* drink, but he had a point: I'd already had some in the car on the way back from Sligo, and it had knocked me right out. Did I *want* to be knocked out?

An image of Brendan's knife, coming towards

Toasted

my eyes, filled my head. I gave a hard shudder, took a deep breath, and swallowed the whiskey in one gulp. It burned on the way down. I coughed.

Milo plucked the tumbler out of my hands and handed it back to Quinn. "Lie down," he instructed me, in a much softer voice. "I'll get yer arm taken care of. You sleep an' forget whatcha saw."

There wasn't a chance in hell of *that* happening, but it was clear from the shaking of my hands that I wasn't going to function for the rest of the night.

"Okay," I said, and as the alcohol began to take effect, I flopped over and closed my eyes.

Mercifully, Brendan didn't follow me this time.

***

I woke in the best place to be: wrapped securely in Milo's arms. Unfortunately, I also had something of a headache, a horrible case of dry mouth, and the weird lingering sense of unease I always have after a vision. Milo's treatment for my complete meltdown had been effective, but it wasn't one I really wanted to adopt.

Carefully, so I didn't wake him, I got up and staggered into the bathroom. I saw he'd bandaged my arm with the tincture treatment. Since for the first time in days, my arm didn't burn and sting, I guessed Brigit's herbs were doing their job.

I gulped down a glass of water and an ibuprofen and crawled back into bed. Milo was still out.

The past few days, Milo had been up before

me and I'd slept like a coma patient for the most part, so I hadn't had an opportunity to watch him sleep. It was nice, lying beside him in the dark, with the dim light from the lamp we'd accidentally left on spilling over his shoulder.

I propped up on an elbow and studied him. Milo's lashes were really long, inky fans against his fair skin, full enough to make any woman jealous. I certainly was. He had a faint scattering of freckles over his nose and cheeks, only really visible this close. A tiny chickenpox scar sat under the corner of his left eye like a reverse beauty mark. His jaw was dark with stubble that felt prickly under my fingers as I touched his cheek.

He did something with his hair during the day so that the curls were somewhat under control, but at the moment they were a riot of dark ringlets, sticking out in all directions. Milo's hair was never anything like an "afro", the curls big and loose, but mussed from sleep.

Wrapping one lock around my finger, I sighed. His hair was softer than mine, the blessing of superb genetics. My hair was stick-straight and frizzed; by rights, he should have been the one to deal with bad hair days, but no, he just had to run his fingers through it and be done.

"Mm." Milo stirred and opened an eye just a bit, so all I could see was a sliver of deep green. "What?"

"I'm going to steal your hair," I whispered. "I haven't figured out how yet."

He snorted and rolled to bury his face in his pillow. He mumbled something into it.

"What was that?"

Milo lifted his head long enough to tell me, "Shaved m'head when I was thirteen."

"Why would you do that?"

He sighed and rolled back over, catching my hand to pull me with him. "'Cause I got made fun of at school for havin' 'girl hair'. When there are only 'bout thirty kids in the entire high school, there's not much imagination involved wi' the bullyin'."

I rested my head on his chest, tracing a random design with a fingertip on the front of his sleeveless shirt. "That's a small school."

"Small community," he told me. "Dunno why they bother havin' different towns up there, really."

"Maybe for convenience? Mom and I went on a drive across the midwest once, to Iowa, with my grandparents, and in . . . Nebraska, I think it was? Saw a sign that said there was a population of twenty in the town. Thing was, it was cornfields as far as the eye could see, and one windmill. No houses, no buildings. Kinda creepy. But out there in the middle of nowhere, it'd be weird to be incorporated into a city farther away."

He made a thoughtful noise.

"We're supposed to go back to the States the day after tomorrow," I said suddenly. "But we don't have this wrapped up."

"Lugh said he'll pay the airline fees for changin' our flight," Milo murmured. "We could stay another week or somethin'."

"Maybe. I feel bad, but I don't want to stay just to deal with this."

He kissed the top of my head and ran his

fingers through my hair. "If we hafta stay, I'll make sure we see more o' the sights, *cailín*. I promise."

"Let's get back to sleep."

"You feelin' okay? Still got a bit of a fever."

Sighing, I looped my arm around his waist. "I think I will 'til the infection is gone. But my arm doesn't hurt so much anymore, so maybe . . . it won't last much longer."

"I hope so," he said, and kissed my forehead.

CHAPTER NINETEEN

After the vision I'd had, I definitely couldn't just walk away from this. I could more easily face the horror I'd seen in the light of day, and I discussed it with Lugh and Milo when we dropped by the *Tuatha*'s abode. Lugh handled the exchange with the airline.

Rhoda wasn't exactly thrilled when I called her from Muriel's to tell her we'd be staying another week, but she understood that sometimes, my life as a medium took precedence over mundane things like my job. And in this case, she was also out Milo for another week, which meant that she was down not one, but two employees. As I hung up the phone, I sighed.

"She not happy we're not on our way back?" Milo asked.

"No, not really. But she understands. I'm so making your dad pay a retainer fee or something," I grumbled.

He snickered. "From the looks a'things, he can afford it."

"You still mad at him?" I asked. "I know it's not my business, but you know me. I'm nosy and curious."

Milo barely managed to refrain from rolling his eyes. I could see it took effort. "It's . . . complicated, aye? He explained he didn't just leave us for near thirty years. So his absence isn't really his fault. Still . . . weird t'suddenly know the man."

Frowning, I scooted my chair closer. "Wasn't his fault, how? How do you disappear for that long and have it not be your fault? Was he in jail or something?"

That got a genuine laugh. "Or somethin'. Don't think there's a jail out there could hold Lugh if he didn't wanna be held. No, he was in their realm. Tir na n'Og."

"For that long, though?"

He shrugged. "Time differential? It's in the legends, but he says it doesn't always happen, an' usually it's t'humans when it does. For him, he was gone three weeks. For Mam, he was gone twenty-seven years."

"Oh, that really sucks." I winced, suddenly feeling bad for the huge, blonde god. It didn't erase that Eithne had been left on her own to raise two children at the age of seventeen, but . . . "I can't imagine coming back to find everything's changed and you have two adult kids."

"Aye, that'd be a hell of a thing."

***

Apparently, Muriel didn't even want to consider opening the shop in the wake of Ciara's death, and she stayed home to work on projects in her studio and package internet orders. She and I went to lunch, just the two of us, after we went grocery shopping. I hadn't ever managed to pick up that milk, after all.

"I'm sorry 'bout last night," she told me as we ate fried haddock and big, thick chips. "Must be horrible, seein' that stuff."

"It's not in any way your fault," I told her. "But I appreciate the sympathy. It . . . wasn't fun. And no, I won't tell you what I saw."

"I don't need t'know," she assured me. "I've read enough- Anyway. I know all I need to. I just feel bad she hasn't been released so her parents can bury her."

"They probably will this week," I said. "Have you spoken to them?"

"Her mam, yeah. This morning. Hateful thing, this whole business. I couldn't stop thinkin' about it while we were in France, though I tried."

"And you wouldn't have appreciated coming home to find out," I said.

"Hell, no," she said vehemently. "I needed t'know, even if it . . . put a damper on things wi' Quinn."

I nodded in understanding. I wasn't about to mention what I'd been doing with Milo when Ciara had appeared to us, but that hadn't been exactly conducive to fun times, either. I still didn't know if I wanted to pursue that, or wait.

Muriel doused her fish with vinegar. "You're thinkin' pretty hard there," she observed.

"Oh, I . . ." My face went red of its own volition. "Weighing the pros and cons of . . . something."

"Shaggin' my brother?" she asked, somewhat gleefully.

My blush only deepened, answer enough.

"I'm s'posed to be the good Catholic girl, aye?" she said, after a moment. "But I wasn't when Quinn came along. Or after he came along, I should say. Fell right inta bed wit'him. We've been together for years, an' only just got married 'cause . . . I dunno, really. Guilt, I guess. Technically speakin', we weren't s'posed t'be livin' together, it bein' in sin an' all that."

"Yeah, I've heard something along those lines. How'd you convince the priest to marry you?"

She laughed, green eyes sparkling. "He said it was 'bout damn time an' that us movin' out temporarily to separate places wasn't gonna change that we've been together so long, so he was just gonna marry us an' make it legal an' lawful."

"I see."

"But what I'm gettin' at is, if ya find yerself weighin' pros an' cons based on others' expectations? Don't do that. Do what feels right t'you. If it ain't right at this moment? Don't do it just 'cause you know he wants to. But," she cautioned, with a finger raised, "don't let what others think hold ya back. It's your life, yeah? An' I get the feelin' that if it's fer religious reasons? Well, all I gotta say 'bout that is, Milo's a Druid."

Yeah, my family might balk at that a little more than my prematurely bonking him.

We finished lunch and did a little window shopping. I didn't have the money to really buy anything, having spent most of my available funds on the dress I'd worn as bridesmaid. I did, however, have a card in my wallet that Lugh had given me for "discretionary spending" in the line of investigation.

I'd asked what "discretionary spending" meant, and he'd just smiled at me.

It was midafternoon by the time we made it back to the O'Donnell house. Milo was in the kitchen, half under the sink, with a wrench, while Quinn crouched beside him with a flashlight.

"Is that leakin' again?" Muriel asked.

"Yer water pressure is shite," Milo grumbled from the depths of the cabinet.

"Tell me somethin' I *don't* know," his sister returned.

I was entranced by the expanse of stomach visible between Milo's rucked-up tee and his low-riding jeans. Muriel saw me looking and snickered, elbowing me a little in the side.

"Oh," she said, after a moment, and reached into her bag.

Muriel handed me a brochure. "Not sure if this is your kinda thing," she said, "but I saw it at the grocer's and brought it back."

"It" was a pamphlet for a ghost tour, conducted by bus, around Dublin. It visited famous sites, included nighttime entrance to some churches, and had two showings a night. Looked interesting, I had to admit.

Milo cursed in Irish. There was a clanking sound, then, "Ha!" He shimmied out from under the sink and sat up.

"Spider in your hair," Quinn told him mildly.

Milo flailed his hands through his curls, making a decidedly girly noise. He knocked the spider to the floor and mashed it repeatedly with the wrench.

"Well," I said, after a moment, "that was manly."

"Ah, shush," he grumbled. He stood, shook himself off, and came over to greet me. Seeing the brochure in my hands, he took it to examine.

"More dead people," he commented.

I had to smile. "It does sound fun, though."

"I was thinkin' maybe the four o'us could go," Muriel put in. "Do somethin' fun for a change. Maybe do dinner, too."

Shrugging, I looked to Milo. "I'm up for it if you are."

"Sure," he said. "Let's do that."

His sister grinned. "Great!"

***

To be honest, I was sick and tired of dead people. But they were part of my daily life, so I couldn't escape them. It made sense to see the lighter side of it as often as I could, and I couldn't escape the appeal of just being a tourist and getting to see places normally off-limits.

We'd had a few nice days of sunshine, but it was shaping up to be a cool evening again, so I dressed in the new jeans and sweater Milo had picked out, and my sturdier walking shoes. As we piled into the car for our double date, I ruminated that if I'd been wearing these, instead of the slip-ons, I might not have lost my shoes in the bog and wandered around barefoot.

Muriel was obviously still bothered by Ciara's death, but seemed determined to not let it ruin her evening. She knew we were doing what we could, and while she hadn't asked yet to speak to Ciara, simply knowing that she *could* appeared to be something of a balm to her.

Milo was good at keeping the mood light and his sister distracted with amusing stories. He was full of them in the car and at the restaurant, though the veracity of several could be disputed.

"He toldja about shaving his head?" Muriel exclaimed at dinner. She laughed. "All those poor girls at school were so crushed when he did that."

Milo pinkened. "I was gawky, too skinny an' too tall, an' I had girl hair!"

I couldn't help snickering. "How, exactly, did your mom react to you shaving your head?"

"Livid," Muriel put in. "Absolutely livid. Not 'cause he did it, mind, but 'cause he didn't tell her he was doin' it. Goes t'school in the morning with a full head of hair, comes back with none o'it."

I grimaced, but had to laugh. "My mom would

have killed me if I'd done something like that. I never even gave myself bangs as a kid. Every haircut had to be discussed into the ground, for at least a week beforehand."

Quinn, silent until now about this turn of conversation, ran a hand over his slightly-balding head. "I went to a Catholic private school, so I had the same haircut 'til I graduated. Almost like a military school, really. Don't think my hair was longer than two centimeters 'til I got to college."

"An' you roomed wi' the culchie musician wi' the long hair," Milo reminded him. "I think yer mam about had an attack when she saw me the first time."

"She nearly did," Quinn agreed, his grin broad.

I poked at my potatoes with my fork, smiling wistfully. I hadn't gone away to college, hadn't had roommates to freak my mother out. And I hadn't been out of college long when I'd lost her to breast cancer. Yeah, she was still around, technically speaking, but it wasn't the same. I didn't have a bunch of friends like this group, didn't have all those fun college memories. Closest I had was Maegan, and she was five thousand miles away.

Milo slid an arm around my shoulders and pressed a kiss to my temple. "You okay?" he whispered.

I had to clear my throat before speaking. "Fine," I replied. "Just tired."

"You wanna skip the tour?"

"No way!"

After dinner, we walked up O'Connell Street to the Dublin Bus headquarters, where we waited. It was a little chilly, damp and drizzly, so I huddled against Milo for warmth.

"Nice, creepy night," Quinn said. "Y'know, I've never done this tour?"

"I did once, with Rose an' Nell," Muriel said. "It was fun."

For once, Ciara wasn't present. That let me relax a little more, which in turn made me feel guilty. I coughed into my hand and cleared my throat for what seemed like the billionth time that evening.

"You gettin' sick?" Milo asked me.

"Maybe. I *did* wander around in the rain for a couple hours the other night, and who knows what was in that tomb?"

A big, primarily purple and black bus--with a mural of ghosts on it--pulled up to the curb. Yellow letters emblazoned on the side informed us it was the "Ghost Bus". We presented our tickets to the driver and piled on with a bunch of tourists, winding our way up a very narrow circular stair to the second level.

Milo and I snagged seats at the very front, with Muriel and Quinn just behind. It was dark inside the bus, with black curtains drawn over the windows.

"I've never ridden a double-decker," I said idly. "When we went to England, Mom leased a car for the duration, so we didn't need public transport."

"What were ya in England for?" Muriel inquired, leaning forward with her arms across the back of the seat.

I twisted around. "My mother was an author, history stuff. She did a book on haunted castles of England when I was twelve."

"Really? That's very cool! You see any

ghosts?"

"Anne Boleyn. I was young enough that I don't know about others. There were a lot of people in period costume around, so I could have spoken to a ghost and not known it. It still happens now and then."

We kept our voices low, mostly because we didn't want to attract any undue attention. You start talking about seeing dead people in public, normal humans tend to start thinking you're nuts or full of it. Sometimes both. I just didn't want to deal with that tonight.

Quinn squinted at Milo in the dim bus interior, then turned that look on me. "What else can you see?" he inquired. "Just ghosts, or . . .?"

I shrugged. "So far, just ghosts. Why?"

"Just wonderin', with everythin' I've learned about my dear wife an' best friend."

Note to self: ask Lugh, next time I see him, what things are real and what aren't.

The tour guide came up and things got underway. Our first "stop"--we didn't even get out of the bus, just peered past the curtains at the building-- was a former medical school where a really macabre doctor performed "autopsies" in front of his students by yanking out organs with his bare hands. He apparently died in the middle of one, having a heart attack. When the guide joked that the doc had been a Godless man, saying "of course he was Godless, he was from Cork", my companions laughed. I didn't get the joke.

We went by Dublin Castle, briefly, and were told that several revolutionaries were rumored to haunt its halls. I hadn't seen a single one while we were there, but that didn't mean anything, on the whole.

Bram Stoker was big on the list, and we went by his former residence. He'd lived in the flat while writing "Dracula". Naturally, we didn't get to go see anything. I was more interested in the hotel where a "famous American psychic" had seen the ghost of a little girl. We'd made our way across the city to St Stephen's Green by this point. It was dark enough that the tour guide let us open the curtains fully.

"See anythin' yet?" Muriel asked in my ear.

"Of course not, we haven't even got off the bus."

If Maegan had been there, I'm sure we would have annoyed the tour guide with all sorts of smart remarks, but I didn't have my partner in crime with me. If I ever came back, I vowed that I would bring Mags along for this tour.

The bus finally let us off on a little side street, where we obediently filed along the sidewalk until we reached a creepy, wrought-iron gate set in an old wall. I peered through the bars into a pitch-black nothingness that reminded me uncomfortably of the darkness outside the cairn where Brendan had held me prisoner. I shivered and Milo pulled me close, tucking me under his arm.

"Welcome to St. Kevin's church," the guide intoned. He went on to inform us, as he let us in, that the property had once held a cemetery, but had been converted into a park. "Mostly," he added. "Some of the bodies didn't get moved."

A couple of young girls shrieked and grabbed

each other, jumping up and down while looking at their feet. I rolled my eyes.

The church's tale was a bit sad, full of death and persecution and a smattering of devil worship. It had burned down centuries ago and stood as a roofless ruin in the south of the city. People had died in the fire, and I felt them around, invisibly watching and waiting.

Quinn hung back, by me, as I took pictures of the mostly-blank headstones. "I wanna thank you, Peyton, for bein' a friend to Muriel."

I blinked up at him, a little blinded by the flash from my camera. "Why wouldn't I be?"

He shrugged. "Some of the girls Milo's dated, well . . . He's my best friend, but up 'til you? He's had piss-poor taste in women."

I snorted a laugh and clapped my hand over my mouth.

"Darcy's Muriel's bestie, so I'd never say anythin' against her," he confided, "but Lord love me, I can't stand the woman."

I made a non-committal noise and snapped another picture.

"So you see the dead, huh? Like that kid in that movie?"

Shrugging, I turned to squint at him in the darkness. Several people in the group had flashlights, so his face was occasionally lit by a beam as it passed over us.

"Something like that, though usually not the ultra-gory stuff. And before you ask, I'm not seeing anyone right now. I'm sure I'm going to get a bazillion orbs in my pictures, because I always do, but I can't see any ghosts." I scanned the darkness around us. "They're here, though. I don't know if they're aware enough to make a real appearance, or if they've sort of lost themselves over time."

"That's fascinatin'."

We made our way along the path, following the others, to the church proper. It had a dirt floor and empty, barred windows. I snapped a few pictures with my flash off, just to see if orbs *did* show up for me.

"I wonder," Quinn said idly, "if these were added before or after the fire? Are they t'keep vandals out? That seems silly, what wi'no roof an' a stone wall ya could climb fairly easy. Or were they t'keep people in?"

"You mean, were they added to keep people inside when the place was set on fire? That's a disturbing thought."

He made a derisive sound somewhere to my left. "That's the English, though. Fond of burnin' people t'death in churches. Didn't they do that in America?"

"I don't actually know. They did in *The Patriot*, but that was a movie."

I became aware that Muriel and her brother were in a low-pitched, somewhat heated discussion, across the church. I didn't want to eavesdrop, but every few words were loud enough that I didn't have to try.

"What?!" she demanded. "That's ridiculous!"

Milo responded in an undertone. I wandered over to the altar and snapped a few pictures. I was intensely curious, but it wasn't any of my business.

"That's a stupid thing t'do, she'll-"

She? I snapped another picture.

"Don't know *how*-" This from Milo.

"Well, ya better figure it, ya eejit."

Then they switched to Gaeilge, and I couldn't decipher anything else.

Quinn scuffed a toe in the dirt. "Probably arguing about Darcy," he put in. "Milo told us she dropped by the other night an' made a pest of herself."

Oh, that made sense. Darcy was a subject Milo and I were studious in avoiding of late. I'd much rather he discuss her with Muriel than with me. I didn't discuss Rob with him, either.

Back on the bus, I found my thoughts turning to Ciara. Why had Brendan chosen *her*, of Muriel's friends? How had he singled her out, rather than say, Rose, or Darcy?

Then it hit me. Darcy had walked with us to her car, in the same garage as Muriel's. Rose and Nell had left together. The only one who had been alone and vulnerable was Ciara. Ciara, who had been stupidly drunk and wandering around Dublin like a lost lamb. Any predator would have singled her out as the weakest of the herd.

And we had to be dealing with a predator, probably a well-verse and practiced one at that. An amateur wouldn't snag a girl off the street without a trace in a city watched over by CCTV, not without leaving some sign of it. It had to be someone who knew Dublin, which Brendan didn't. Oh, he might know landmarks, he'd been awake long enough for that, but to memorize the nooks and crannies in a city that had sprung up long after he'd gone to sleep in that dolmen? No. We were dealing with someone who was street-smart, savvy, who knew where the cameras were, knew how people saw what they expected to see, especially late at night in Temple Bar.

"What's got you thinkin' so hard?" Milo asked, nudging me with his elbow.

"Ciara. Or, rather, her kidnapper."

"Take a break, aye?"

"Trying."

Our next stop was St. Audoen's, near the old boundary of the city, a big church built into the old city wall. The guide told us of the entrance to "Hell", a city-sized brothel and gambling den that had existed in the tunnels under the city. The madame of the brothel, one Darky Kelly, executed for supposedly killing her own child, one she'd really just given to the nuns of the church. She'd been hung and set on fire on the gates of the church.

"Some days you can see the Green Lady wandering these steps," the tour guide said, shining his flashlight up a long staircase that curved around the side of the church.

I glanced over at the gates, where a woman in a green dress leaned against the wall, looking bored. "No, she's over by the gate," I said aloud.

Everyone stopped and looked at me.

Milo made an amused sound under his breath.

"What?" the guide asked, aiming the light at me.

"Um." Crap. What now? Lie, make something up, tell the truth? "The ghost? They tend to haunt where they died, don't they? So if she died at the gates, why would she be seen on the stairs?"

Darky Kelly wandered over to me, looking me up and down. She was pretty, in her own way, but obviously hard-used and of poor hygiene. Her dark hair, the source of her appellation, hung in untidy ringlets around her shoulders. "You can see me, can't ya, girlie? Ain't that somethin'."

"That might be," the tour guide said, oblivious to Darky's presence, "but rumour says . . ."

He wandered off towards the stairs, dismissing me entirely.

"Yes," I said to the ghost, in a low voice. "I can see you. Why are you still here?"

"'Cause it's fun t'scare the nice little biddies inna church," she said, with a broad grin that revealed a few missing teeth. "I sometimes wander up the stairs, aye, but mostly, I'm here by the gate. People see me on occasion, but not like you. You're special, ain'tcha?"

"I can see you, too," Milo put in.

Darky turned his way, eyes widening. "Oh, ye're a pretty one! If I were still alive, I'd give you a toss fer free."

"He's taken," I told her. "So, you're okay with being here? Haunting this church?"

"An' the tunnels," she told me cheerfully. "An' I'm not the only one here. Graveyard's full o' people I talk to. You askin' if I wanna 'move on'? Nah. Thanks, though."

"This . . . might be a personal question, but . . . The child you gave up, was it a boy or a girl?" I asked quietly.

"A girl." Darky looked over at the church and sighed.

"Did you get to see her grow up?"

A smile lit her face. "I did. She never saw me, but she grew up right here. Never followed the path I took. Considered takin' her vows, she did, but she married a farmer out Dingle way an' had three lovely babies. Never knew I was her mam, buit that's a'right."

She looked Milo over again, dark eyes sly, then sidled up to me and whispered a truly obscene suggestion in my ear. I blushed furiously, something only she could see, and she cackled madly before going off through the bricked-up entrance to the underground.

Muriel and Quinn had been watching this exchange in silence. "What," Quinn asked, "just happened?"

I sighed. "Ghost," I said. "You wanted a ghost tour. Well, you got one."

CHAPTER TWENTY

Milo and I were helping out by doing the dishes when his cell rang. He dried his hands on one of the kitchen towels before he fetched the phone from his back pocket. I continued scrubbing while he stepped away to take the call.

I hate doing the dishes. I usually put them off as long as possible, usually until I run out of spoons. Having someone to keep me company while I washed up helped. Not that Milo was doing much assisting at the moment.

The dishes were drying when Milo came back into the kitchen, with a broad smile tinged with concern. I tucked the towel back on the rack to dry before I asked, "What's up?"

"Angus is back in town, gatherin' of pagans this weekend, and he wondered if I wanted t'join him for a drink."

Shrugging, I replied, "If you want to go, then go and have fun. I'll stick close to the house. I think Muriel said she's staying in, so I won't be alone."

The longer it went without another appearance from Brendan, the more I began to relax. It was quite possible I wouldn't be a jumpy, nervous wreck by the time we left.

"You sure?"

"I'm sure, yeah. I mean, when's the last time you saw the guy and really got to hang out? Christmas?"

Milo threaded his fingers through the hair at the back of my head and bent to give me a quick, hard kiss that took my breath. "Thanks, *cailín*."

He loped off into the corridor, calling, "I'm takin' the car for a bit!" to his sister.

"Don't wreck it!" was all she said.

Laughing under my breath, I drained the sink and dried my hands. Muriel padded in on stocking feet and said, "So he's ditched ya for the evening. Never thought I'd see that."

"He's going for a drink with Angus."

"Ahh. I could use one meself," the taller woman admitted. "Maybe in coffee. I'm feelin' run down."

She prepared herself a mug, heavy on cream and whiskey, and offered me some cocoa. I accepted, and we moved into the parlor. Quinn was in the office, doing some bookkeeping work of some sort. Math was not my strong suit; thank heavens I had an uncle who made a living as an accountant.

Sitting on the sofa, I drew my legs up and wrapped both hands around the warm mug of chocolate. My feet were killing me, though the blisters no longer oozed. The mess on my wrist was looking better, too, after just one dose of Brigit's tincture.

"I get the feeling," Muriel said slowly, "you're not real fond of Angus."

I grimaced. "I'd hoped I wasn't that transparent. I just don't know the guy, and he was . . . kind of a jerk to me at your wedding."

"Mm." She folded her long legs under her and eyed me over her own mug. "He's a possessive lad, Angus. Not really one for makin' friends, even when we were kids. Mam wasn't thrilled when Milo took up wit' him, but there wasn't much she could say to a fourteen-year-old who was already a head taller'n her."

"I just get the feeling Angus disapproves of me."

"He probably worries you're takin' Milo away. When Milo lived here in Dublin, wasn't so bad, yeah? Just a few hours' drive, or an hour from the Donegal airport. But now he's in America, and I think Angus probably worries you're gonna keep 'im."

I took a sip of cocoa and considered that. "I'd like to," I admitted. "Keep him."

Her green eyes were serious and focused on me with an uncomfortable intensity. Muriel's dark curls spilled around her shoulders, frothy and a little wild. "Good. 'Cause I love me brother. I want him to be happy, and he's been the happiest I've ever seen since he met you. I'd be very upset if ya broke his heart, Peyton."

"I'd sooner cut off a limb," I murmured. "I love him so much, it scares me sometimes. My biggest fear used to be, like, spiders. Now it's losing him."

I paused. "And getting buried alive in a peat bog, but . . ."

She made a face. "I'm glad you're a'right," she told me. "I near had a heart attack when Milo told us what'd happened. I can't believe the horrible things that've happened the past few days."

"I have to say," I commented, "you and Quinn have taken it all a lot better than I would have expected, for devout Catholics."

She ran a long finger around the rim of her mug. I noted that like her brother, her ring finger was as long as the middle. When she didn't respond, I thought maybe I'd stirred something I shouldn't have.

"Sorry, I didn't mean to-"

"Nah, s'alright. I guess it's cause I've always felt somethin' was off about meself, y'know? I learned too fast at school, was much more skilled at things earlier'n I shoulda been." Muriel held up her right hand, showed me a gorgeously-wrought silver ring. "Made this in high school, on a whim. It's what got me started makin' jewels. Took some classes in college. I never made mistakes like t'others did. Painting, jewellery, sculpture, it all worked the first time I set my hands to the material. That ain't normal, Peyton."

Given that my sole attempt at jewelry-making had been a mixed design class in high school and had resulted in lumpy enamelled beads and a horribly burned finger the day before Prom, I had no real experience with that. When I told her, she laughed hysterically.

"I woulda loved to burn me fingers," she confessed. "Make me feel like less of a freak, aye?"

"I understand the freak thing," I said ruefully. "But why's Quinn taking this so well?"

She shrugged. "He's known us years, for one. I'd say Milo's more obviously fey than me, his ears are pointier, an' Quinn roomed wit' him in school. But he told me . . . if it was a choice between me an' a messed-up family, or no me an' a normal, boring life, he'd choose me every time. Not sure how much of this all he actually believes, but . . ."

"He loves you, and is willing to accept the quirks if it means keeping you."

"Exactly."

We shared a look of understanding. I, too, was Christian and struggling with the oddities of Milo's paternal relations and everything that came along.

Ciara meandered in, trailing ghostly fingers over--and through--various knickknacks scattered around the room. I followed her progress with my eyes, but didn't want to alarm Muriel.

She was too perceptive, though. "She's here, isn't she?" Muriel whispered.

I could only nod.

The ghost couldn't move things, but she'd learned to "sit", so far as a spirit actually can. I don't know how they do it, and it's always felt rude to ask.

"Can I speak t'her?" my boyfriend's sister asked.

Ciara turned to look at us. Sad to say, I was kind of used to the eyeless sockets by now. Maybe I was just in shock and saving the screaming hysterics for when it was all over, because *yeesh*, she was difficult to look at.

"We can try," I allowed. "She's more coherent now than she's been. More aware of people and her surroundings. But I wouldn't . . . ask about what happened, she gets . . ."

The only word I could think of to explain it was "fragmented", but it was really difficult to explain to someone who couldn't see, hear, or feel Ciara.

Finally, I settled on, "Upset. She gets upset."

"Wouldn't you?" Muriel asked pragmatically. "So how do we do this?"

"Well . . . This would be so much easier if you could see her like Milo can."

Muriel leaned over and set her mug on the coffee table. "I think I could," she said softly. "When I was little. See things. But it scared me. Like . . . Mam's house is old, couple centuries, an' there was this woman'd walk the halls an' beg fer help. I ignored her 'til I stopped seein' her."

That was interesting. "So you, what, blocked it all out?"

She nodded. "An' took refuge in God. Thought for sure I was bein' tormented by devils." Muriel thought for a moment, added, "Not sure I was that far off."

I finished my cocoa and put the mug beside hers. "There have been times I've wished I could turn it off, but I can't. No amount of wishing or praying has made my abilities go away. So I've learned to live with it."

Indicting the ghost, I said, "Ciara's a bit different for me, though. She . . . doesn't look the same as others I've seen. Well, Anne Boleyn excluded, but that's because the queen likes to carry her head around. Ciara's, um . . . She was hurt and . . . I can see her . . . trauma. I don't want to tell you about it. You really don't want or need to know."

Muriel considered that for a long, silent moment. "Alright. I'll trust yer judgment, since you're the expert."

Expert, ha! my Inner Voice put in.

I told it to shut up.

"So how's this work?" Muriel inquired. She leaned back against the arm of the sofa and tipped her head in a way that reminded me eerily of her brother.

"Basically, I convey what she says to you. I don't have to play interpreter both ways, she can hear you just fine."

Those green eyes widened almost imperceptibly and flicked around the room for several seconds, as if she was trying to locate her ghostly friend. I gestured towards the front window. Ciara was fond of windows, I guess to watch the things she couldn't interact with anymore.

"She's over there, by the window. Ciara?"

The ghost turned. I still had to force myself not to flinch. Was I never going to get used to seeing her like that? And why *was* I seeing it? Man, I wished I had someone to ask about it.

"Muriel wants to talk to you," I explained to

the spirit. "I'm gonna be your go-between, since she can't see or hear you, okay?"

After a moment, Ciara nodded. "Best she can't see me. I know what I look like now. Look on your face says it all."

"Sorry," I murmured. Clearing my throat, I asked, "So . . . who wants to start?"

I really hate this stuff, I do. It's so awkward being the third wheel for a conversation between people that, realistically, I should have no part in. It's one of the reasons I refuse to do seances. I'm not good at emotional stuff, especially others' emotions.

"I'm sorry you missed my wedding," Muriel said. "Stupid thing to say, right? But I am. You shoulda been there. Shoulda been safe, with us."

"You couldn't help it," Ciara said. "You couldn't know I was missin', an' that man-"

She broke off and shuddered, while I repeated her words to the brunette curled beside me.

"We should have made sure ya reached home safe," Muriel insisted.

"I did," Ciara told us. "Went back out, though, didn't I? Bloody stupid thing t'do, pissed as I was."

"Why *did* you go back out?" I asked her.

The ghost rolled her shoulders in a surprisingly elegant shrug, given her horrific appearance. "Figured the bouncer wouldn't call, wanted a boy in me bed. I . . . I dunno where he grabbed me. I don't . . . *remember* much b'tween leavin' the flat an' wakin' up . . . *there*."

I knew what she meant by "there", now, and it brought a moment of panic back as I recalled what she'd gone through. Taking deep breaths, I drew my legs further up onto the sofa, as if curling into a ball would help.

"What *can* you remember?" Muriel asked her friend quietly. "Anythin' at all."

Ciara paced from the window to the door, and back, pulling at her hair. "I jes'- Lightnin'? No, no. Zig-zags. Or- What's that called, the fabric wit' the squiggles, all tweedy?"

"Herringbone?" I suggested.

She pointed at me. "That, yeah! Herringbone. I dunno why, I just keep seein' it. An St Brigid's Cross. Though, we've met her an' I wouldn't say she's much of a saint."

I didn't translate the last part of that comment to Muriel. "St Brigid's Cross? That star-shaped thing with all the wrapping in the middle?"

Ciara nodded. "Those two things keep comin' back t'me, though I dunno why."

We were quiet for a while. Muriel excused herself to fetch me some more cocoa, and herself a straight shot of whiskey. I let this new information bounce around in my head, pondering the meaning.

"Herringbone jacket, maybe?" I suggested, as Muriel handed me the refreshed mug.

Muriel tossed back her shot of whiskey and made a face. "Ugly as sin, herringbone jackets."

"No idea," Ciara said. "Why can't I see his face?"

"Trauma," I told her. "And maybe you didn't see *his* face, just Brendan's."

She sighed explosively and kicked out at the coffee table. The shot glass Muriel had just put down jumped at the impact and slid an inch or two.

Muriel stared at the table with huge eyes, face gone completely white.

"Did-"

"Ciara kicked the table," I told her. "Some ghosts, especially angry ones, learn to move things. Some, like my mother, never really get a handle on it. I think it has to do with excess energy and stuff."

The ghost, meanwhile, blinked her empty eyes at the table. "Cool," she said, in a hushed voice. "How angry do I gotta be t'move stuff?"

"Uh . . . No idea. I'd prefer if you didn't have a tantrum, though," I told her quickly. "Things can get really messy if you do."

My ex-boyfriend Rob, in every sense of the word, had picked up a huge pottery wheel and smashed my attacker with it back in October. I'd really prefer not to see a repeat of that.

Ciara sat down on the floor, dragging her fingers through her long, dark hair. "S'all I can remember, sorry," she said after a long silence. Everythin's fuzzy b'fore I woke up . . . there."

"It's okay," I assured her. "We'll keep trying."

But I wasn't sure if she had anything else to give us. I hoped the Gardai had found something in the truck with Jennifer's body, or we were really screwed.

CHAPTER TWENTY-ONE

Milo seemed subdued when he came back from his night out with Angus. Though he smelled faintly of Guinness, he wasn't drunk. I suspected it took more than a beer or two to intoxicate one of the *Tuatha Dé Danann*. I actually couldn't ever recall seeing Milo drunk, when I thought about it.

"Have fun?" I asked when he came in. I was reclining on the bed with a Seanan McGuire book, already in my pajamas.

"Mm." He stood in the doorway for a moment, lost in thought. "Hey, at Mure's weddin', did Angus say anythin' to ya?"

"About what? After I mentioned I'm Christian, he didn't say another word to me at all."

Milo nodded and kicked off his shoes.

"M'gonna take a shower, I smell like a pub floor."

Something was bothering him, but I wasn't about to pester him into telling me. I didn't want to get yelled at again. Once had been more than enough.

Contrary to previous nights, he used the bathroom down the hall, rather than the one attached to my room. When he came back, he picked up his shoes.

"You be okay sleepin' here by yerself?" he asked. "I got a lot on me mind an' I dunno how well I'm gonna sleep. I don't wanna disturb ya."

I frowned and sat up a little more, closing the book. "Did I do something?"

He sighed and crossed to the bed, shaking his head. His damp curls hung to his shoulders, turning the shoulders of his grey tee dark. "No, *cailín*, not at all. M'just . . . Had some words wi' Angus an' I need some space, is all."

Milo leaned over and kissed me. "'Sides, we gotta get usedta sleepin' apart again, don't we?"

"I guess." I wasn't at all sure I was ever going to get used to not having him beside me, now that I'd had him there. "Go sleep. I'll be fine. And . . . I'm sorry you fought with your friend."

"Thanks. G'night."

I'd lied. I wasn't fine. It took me forever to fall asleep by myself, and I was plagued by nightmares 'til dawn.

***

Milo was at the stove, making breakfast, when I came down in the morning. I felt lethargic after my restless night, and my boyfriend didn't seem to be faring much better. Muriel was at the kitchen table, doing something with silver chain and little, dark blue beads when I sat down.

"What are you making?" I asked her.

She arched a brow at me, then nodded her head towards Milo. I shook my own, and she frowned. I put my finger to my lips. She rolled her eyes.

"I'm makin' a bracelet," she informed me, and showed me the lengths of chain she'd been measuring and cutting. It was the thinnest, most delicate box chain I'd ever seen, not even a millimeter wide. She had five or six lengths cut, and as I watched, she measured another and snipped it.

I picked up one of the beads, rolling it in my fingers. "What are these?"

"Sapphires from India. Not gem quality, mind, but they'll do. Gonna string 'em on these, bunch 'em together."

"Wow. That'll be pretty." I put the bead back, careful not to knock any to the floor. "So where's Quinn?"

"Went t'the shop," she said. "I don't sell the stuff, anyway, figured I could keep workin' from home while he does the wheelin' an' dealin'. 'Least for the next couple days. Heard from Ciara's mam real early this morning. They're releasin' the body, funeral's on Friday. Murphys aren't Catholic, so there's no Mass t'be said for her."

Milo finished with the food and brought three plates to the table. Muriel moved her bead board to

Quinn's empty chair. "We can go if ya like," he said to me.

"I'd like to," I admitted. "But I . . . I don't want to do the whole message-from-dead-your-loved-one routine."

"Mrs. Murphy's atheist," Muriel told me. "Wouldn't fly well, anyway."

Well, that was something of a relief.

***

After breakfast, Milo informed me that we were going to go on an excursion, and that I was to pack clothes for overnight.

"And *where* are we going?" I asked, as I laced on my walking shoes.

"County Cork," he said. "After that's a surprise."

Oh . . . kaaaaay.

I grabbed my toiletries kit, stuffed some clothes in the pack Muriel loaned me, and my purse. "How are we getting there?" I asked Milo, as we prepared to leave the house.

He dug a card identical to mine, emblazoned with "*Caomhnú Éire*", out of his pocket. "Rentin' one. Da's dime."

"I was told it was for 'discretionary spending'."

"Man's got more money than God," Milo scoffed. Then he paused. "Wait. If he *is* a god . . ."

I shook my head. "Too early for this kind of thing. Makes my brain hurt."

He laughed. "C'mon. We'll take the bus t'pick up a rental."

The bus was a pretty fast ride, all things considered, and within an hour, we had secured a stupidly small car with a surprising amount of head and leg room.

The drive through the countryside in mid-morning was lovely. Everything was all misty still, and lambs frolicked in the fields around their very patient mothers. Everything was so *green*, it almost hurt to look at.

"Okay, so Brendan's here and all, but . . . I almost don't want to go back to the States," I told him as we drove. "It's so . . . peaceful here."

"I miss it a lot, though it's lovely where we are," Milo said.

"Why *did* you move to Utah? Not that I'm complaining, because if you hadn't, we wouldn't have met."

Green eyes slanted my way briefly before he looked back at the road. "Uh. That's a complicated thing."

"Well, we've got several hours ahead of us," I pointed out.

He sighed and drummed his fingers on the steering wheel, still not answering.

"Milo."

"Ah, a'right! I went 'cause I was havin' dreams 'bout it."

I turned in my seat to look at him, skepticism written all over my face, I'm sure. "You moved five thousand miles and across an ocean because of a *dream*?"

Milo shook his head. "Wasn't just a dream, aye? It was . . . It was drivin' me *mad*, havin' it every bloody night. An' I'd just found out about Lugh, an' all. Decided I wanted t'get away. Mike offered t'put me up."

"Must have been some dream," I commented. "What was it about, exactly?"

"Nope, that one's for another day, *cailín*. A man needs his secrets."

"Okay, fine. But it's just going to drive *me* crazy now, wondering."

He grinned.

The car had a hookup for Milo's smartphone, and we listened to his music on the drive. It was an eclectic mix of '80s European rock, Celtic, classical, and modern pop. His tastes were similar to mine, though he had a lot of stuff in his playlist I'd never heard of.

"What's this?" I inquired of one particular song.

"Snow Patrol."

"I've . . . vaguely heard of them. Are they new?"

He snorted. "To America. They've been around f'years."

Eventually, the countryside all began to look the same. We stopped to fill up the car, and I wandered into the attached convenience store. Inside, I found a tiny jug of milk, only holding a pint, but it had a cap and an itty-bitty handle and everything.

"Look at this!" I exclaimed to Milo, holding it up in excitement. "It's so little!"

He plucked it out of my hand and set it back in the cooler. "If we bought everyt'in' you thought was cute jes' 'cause it's small . . ."

I pouted and snatched it back. "And it's chocolate! I'm getting it. I can . . . fill it with something."

An older man in a tweed flatcap nearby chuckled, as he put a lid on his coffee. His dark eyes twinkled as he squinted at us from the depths of deep crow's feet. "Next it'll be wee kittens, an' then a wee cottage. Just don't get her a wee rock, boyo, or ye'll ne'er hear the end o' it."

I snickered as Milo blushed. "Fine," he said, "ya can have the damned milk."

It being only a pint, I had the little jug drained before we'd gone a mile. Milo looked somewhere between amused and frustrated when I stuck it in my bag, but he kept his comments to himself.

We passed through Cork and left the highway for a smaller road. Our little car bumped along, and I found myself longing for the stability of the behemoth that he and Lugh had fetched me from Sligo in. This tiny car was one exception to my thought that small equaled cute.

"Please tell me that wherever we're going, we'll be there soon," I said. I barely held in a groan as the car rocked sideways.

"Accordin' t' the GPS, it's just two kilometers that way." Milo gestured through the windshield.

"This had better be worth the seasickness," I muttered.

"Oh, it will be."

Milo pulled the car off the road and parked where the GPS indicated, and we got out. I saw . . . nothing. Trees, some gorse--stuff I never wanted to get near again, *ever*--wildflowers, and lots of grass.

". . . We drove, what, two hundred miles for . . . *this*?" I couldn't contain my disappointment. "Where *are* we?"

He held out his hand. "Close yer eyes. I'll guide ya."

Reluctantly, I did as directed, placing my hand in his much larger one. Uncertain as I was, his grip on my hand was reassuring.

"If you let me fall in a ravine, I'll kill you," I grumbled.

Milo laughed. "Just go slow. I won't let ya fall."

I'm not sure how long we walked, but it was a fair distance from the road, down an incline and around at least one hill. I was dying of curiosity by the time Milo stopped, tugging on my hand to signal me.

"Alright," Milo said. "Open yer eyes."

I did, blinking in the afternoon sunlight. Then I gasped.

Spread before me, on a crest of a low hill that overlooked a rolling valley, was a standing stone circle. It wasn't tall and extravagant like Stonehenge, but it was all the more incredible for its humble grace.

"Oh. Wow. Milo, it's amazing! Where are we? Does it have a name or anything?"

Grinning, he pulled me into the ring of stones. "Carrigagulla."

I laughed. "Seriously? I swear, all these names are made up just to make the English get tongue-tied."

"Partially," he chuckled. "There are some rings closer t'Dublin, but I wanted t'show ya this one in particular."

Enthralled, I spun around. "I love it!"

I spent a good fifteen minutes snapping picture after picture, exploring all the stones from different angles. I'd seen Stonehenge from a distance, when I was young, but it had nothing on this one, at least to me.

Milo sat on a boulder that occupied the center of the circle, watching me as I wandered around. Finally, I joined him there.

"Good idea, was it?" he asked me.

"Wonderful idea! Thanks for this." I leaned my head against his shoulder.

He wrapped both arms around me and rested his chin on the top of my head. "Looks like no one's done a fertility ritual here in ages," he commented. "Grass is a bit brown an' sparse."

"What does a fertility ritual entail?" I asked curiously.

His laugh shook us both. "I'd demonstrate, but we'd both need t'be nekkid."

"Oh? Skyclad ritual?"

Milo snorted. "No. Fertility ritual, 'least like I'm thinkin' of, would be, uh . . . you an' me, or whoever the man an' woman happened t'be . . . y'know. Here, on this altar."

I laughed in surprise. "Really? Actual sex magic?"

"Mm-hmm. I been to one. Awkward as hell, that was."

I scuffed my toe in the first. "I think I'll pass

on the ritual, at least for now."

Milo kissed my temple. "For now?" he repeated.

"Well, you know. One day, I . . . I want to . . . I'm just not ready."

"I'm not gonna push."

"I can't tell you how much I appreciate that."

We sat there and watched the sun dip lower in the sky, not really doing much of anything. It was really nice to just relax and get away. There were no spirits here, just some birds chattering away as they flitted to and fro in the air above us.

"So what kind of rituals would have been done here?" I asked.

"Oh, all sorts."

"Sacrifices?"

"Not human. Never human, unless it was the enemy an' it was . . ." He shrugged. "Hard to explain, aye? Druids didn't do all that crap the Romans wrote about, wi' the wicker people an' stuff. The Saxons may have, I dunno, but us? No. Sure, we had executions an' all, but never human sacrifice t'appease the gods."

I stood and stretched my legs. My feet still hurt, but I didn't mind so much here. "What, no crazies doing it?"

"Oh, I'm sure there were some crazies doin' it," he told me. "Aren't there always? But officially? Not done. Da wouldna put up wit' it."

"You sound really sure of that, considering you've only known him a few days."

"I asked him. When we were at his flat, an' you were nappin' wi' the dog."

"Oh."

He stood and took my hand. "Ready t'go?"

"Yeah, I guess. Are we going back to Cork?"

"Best place to find a hotel. You saw the wide spot inna road we passed through? That was the nearest 'town' t' Carrigagulla."

"Ugh."

CHAPTER TWENTY-TWO

It was a bit of a hike back to the car, and my feet ached again. My arm, however, had made vast improvements and barely hurt.

He started the car, startling a doe grazing on a nearby bush, and she leapt across the road, white tail flashing.

"Tell me about St. Brigid's Cross," I said.

Milo arched a dark brow in my direction. "Why the sudden interest?"

I realized I'd forgotten to share what Ciara had told me the night before. I relayed the new information to him, and he pondered it as he guided the car back towards the main road.

"Brigid's cross," Milo murmured. "Ah . . . Largely a Catholic thing, represents St. Brigid, who got mixed up wit' my cousin Brigit."

"Yeah, I know that the Christians adopted a bunch of the Irish gods and goddesses in an attempt to convert the Celts."

He nodded. "Aye. The cross is s'posed ta represent the saint, anyway. But it's adapted from a sunwheel, usually made outta rushes or straw, an' it's woven."

"Oh, so it's that weird, squarish cross with the arms offset?"

"Yep, that'd be it. There's a story 'bout the saint makin' a cross wi' rushes while tendin' a dyin' Celtic chieftain, but it's also s'posed to protect a house from fire, which ain't part of anythin' St. Brigid ever did, far as I know. They're all over everywhere, as you've seen." He ran his hands over the steering wheel, lost in thought for a while.

I leaned my head back against the headrest. "So . . . maybe wherever she was taken from had one? Or . . . I didn't see one where she was killed. And *that* was local to Dublin, not Brendan's lair in the bog. He didn't have time to get her from Sligo to Dublin for his errand boy to dump her in the park, not if he was in Enniskerry that same night. Even if the freak has wings and can fly, there isn't enough time."

I really, really hoped I never saw that place in person. Just the thought of it scared the hell out of me.

Milo slowed the car for a stray sheep in the road, and honked at it. It gave him an indignant look and slowly shuffled out of the way. "I agree. But there was plenty o' time fer him to get from Enniskerry back t' Dublin from when we saw him at the reception, before he killed 'er."

And we knew precisely when *that* had been, though neither of us brought that up.

"So where was the *saint* from?" I asked him.

"Kildare, I think? She's one'a the patron saints of Ireland."

"And where is that?"

"We drove through it on the way here," he informed me. "It's right next t'County Dublin."

"Could that be where he held her and killed her?" I wondered aloud.

Milo shrugged. "Beats the hell outta me."

The drive back to Cork took nearly an hour. I love the Irish countryside. I loathe the stupidly low speed limits. They made sense in this area, though, because the road was barely paved, let alone wide enough to be considered a highway.

We weren't far from the city when I noticed a sign I'd somehow missed on the way out. "Blarney?" I squeaked, turning in my seat to look at him. "As in Blarney Castle?"

Milo smirked, but didn't say anything as he flipped on the blinker and turned left on the road to the castle. I was a little disappointed to see there were a lot of tourists milling about. We paid our tour "donation" and trudged up the steps of the grey stone castle.

"By the way," Milo began, as we reached the area where the infamous Blarney Stone was, "don't kiss-"

"-the stone, yeah. Every tour book I read mentioned not to do it. And three separate shop clerks the other day said it when I was out with

Muriel. Do guys really pee on it?"

He gestured to where one youth was attempting to surreptitiously unzip his fly. He hadn't managed to expose anything when the security guard grabbed him. We watched in silence as the teenager was hauled back down the stairs, getting an earful the whole way.

". . . Okay. I think I've seen enough."

I took the obligatory pictures, but I'd liked Dublin Castle more, and the architecture here couldn't compare to Kilkenny. We wandered by Blarney House on the way out, a Gothic Revival Victorian mansion on the grounds that I liked much better. Of course, I have a weakness for Victorian houses, which partially came from living in one.

Back in the car, we continued on to Cork. The city was near Bantry Bay, the Atlantic ocean a blue expanse visible from the window of the room we got at a lovely manor house on a hilltop overlooking the city and the bay.

"Are you sure your dad won't mind paying for this?" I asked. I dropped my pack on the bed.

Milo wandered over to the door out to the garden and tested the locks. "While you were inna bathroom, he told me t'take ya somewhere nice an' 'bed ya to make my claim solid'."

I wanted to be offended, but knew the time Lugh came from, and couldn't find indignation in me. Mostly, I just came up with a weak embarrassment. "Him, Muriel, Mags . . ."

Milo drew the curtains closed. "We're not doin' things to anyone's schedule but ours, aye?"

"Right."

"C'mon. Let's go down t' the beach fer a bit. Then, I booked a surprise for ya before dinner."

I arched a brow. "Oh, really?"

"You'll hafta wait an' see," was all he'd tell me.

***

I washed out my little jug and took it with me down to the beach. The bay in Dublin wasn't really accessible and mostly populated by industrial buildings: warehouses, shipyards, and the like. Bantry Bay had docks and ocean-front hotels and restaurants. It was still a little too chilly to take our shoes off, but I picked up a few shells and filled my jug with sand from the beach, determined to take it back to the States with me.

Our hotel had a luxury spa attached, and I was shocked to discover, when we returned from the beach, that Milo had booked me a massage and mani-pedi.

"Don't argue," he said. "My father owes ya a hell of a lot more'n this, an' I want ya coming back from Ireland wit' more good memories than bad."

I couldn't argue with that, so I wandered down to the spa, and spent the rest of the afternoon getting pampered. I hadn't realized how sore and stiff I was from everything until the massage therapist clucked and fussed over the knots in my back and shoulders.

By the time I got to the mani-pedi, I was feeling thoroughly wrung out. The manicurist, who introduced herself as Caitlin, made the same noises the therapist had when she saw the state of my hands.

She was even more distressed when she saw the now-healing wound on my arm. "I can't massage that," she told me.

"I don't expect you to," I assured her. "I just burned myself on a pot in the kitchen, it's nothing contagious."

Caitlin wrinkled her nose, but proceeded to file and paint my nails. Of course, she had another fit when she saw my feet.

"*What*," she demanded, "did ya *do* t' yerself?!"

"It's a really long story, but my boyfriend and I got lost, and then I lost my shoe, and had to walk a couple miles barefoot. You should have seen them last week."

It was kind of funny the way she scolded me about "proper foot health". I got a hot oil soak and a massage, and all the horrible, crusty dead skin filed away. My feet were tender where the blisters had been, but they'd healed the fastest of my various injuries.

When I rejoined Milo, meeting him back at our room, I had my nails painted a sparkly pink. It was obvious that he didn't really care what color they were, but he went through the motions of admiring them anyway.

The hotel's restaurant required reservations, which we didn't have. Lugh's money had got us a room, but the restaurant was small and there weren't any free tables. Milo had tried, but failed. On our way out to find a place to eat, we peered into the dining room, took one look at all the crystal and fancy tablecloths, and decided it was too rich for our tastes, anyway.

"Did you see the place settings?" I asked as we got to the car. "There were, like, six forks."

"I'm simple," he said, "I only need one fork."

"Places like that make me feel like some feral wolf-child. Give me pizza or french fries over boiled snails and artichokes."

He quirked a brow. "Is that what they were servin'?"

"Escargot and artichoke hearts in wine sauce," I confirmed. "Menu's posted outside the door."

"Disgusting. I wonder who discovered snails are edible, anyway? Musta been real desperate t'look at one an' think, 'Oh, that wee, slimy thing looks delicious! I'll fry it in butter.'"

I buckled my seatbelt. "There are places in the States where you can buy deep-fried butter sticks."

Milo twisted in his seat and stared at me, green eyes wide. "Please tell me you're jokin'."

"Sadly, no. And, apparently, deep-fried cans of Coke, though I really have to wonder how *that* works. Do you lick the batter off the can, then drink it? Wouldn't that boil the soda and make it all flat and nasty?"

He shook his head. "An' here I thought the English ate weird crap."

"Mom tried to get me to eat blood pudding when we were in England. I wouldn't touch it."

He pulled out of the small, private parking lot and we headed down the hill to the city. We passed a house with an orange tabby sitting in the window, and I realized it was the first cat I'd seen the whole trip.

"Do people just not have pet cats here?" I

asked. "That's the only one I've seen this entire time."

"I dunno," he said with a frown, glancing in the rear-view though he couldn't see the animal. "I hadn't noticed."

"It's all dogs. Lots of dogs, especially in Dublin. That's really weird."

We decided to park and wander around 'til we found something appealing. It didn't take very long, as there were plenty of places. Cork was, according to Milo, the second-largest city in Ireland. I was a little disappointed, to be honest, by how metropolitan the place was. I'd been hoping for more local charm, not three McDonald's and a Burger King within six blocks of the car.

We settled for a place that offered "modern Irish cuisine". That translated to roast chicken with mashed potatoes and veggies drowned in butter for me, and a positively massive sirloin steak for Milo. Even he seemed surprised by the size of the steak when it arrived. His came with a mound of chunky-cut "chips", similar to what we called steak fries in the US, and I stole a few.

"Ew, mushrooms," I commented, looking at his plate.

He speared one with a fork and threatened me with it. When I recoiled, he laughed and popped the thing in his mouth.

"Found the trick t'keep ya from stealin' me chips at last," he said with satisfaction. "Cover 'em in mushrooms."

I stuck my tongue out at him.

The restaurant wasn't what I'd call "cozy". It

was packed to the rafters, people crammed around every small table, and the decor was a little stark. But the food more than made up for it, and the staff was very friendly. The waitress didn't even hit on Milo, which raised the star rating I was going to give the place online by one whole star by itself. I mean, she *looked*, obviously, but so did most of the women in the restaurant, and a few of the men. Staff that understood boundaries was a rare gift.

A portion of flour-less chocolate cake with cream and a fruit compote was my desert. Milo declined having anything himself, opting to finish his beer instead.

"You really like your chocolate, don't ya?" he asked with amusement as we walked back to the car.

"Mmm. Ply me with enough of it and I'll do anything you ask," I joked.

He grinned. "I'll keep that in mind."

Milo came around to open my door, but before he did, he backed me against it and dipped his head to kiss me. No matter how many times he did, it always left me slightly discombobulated. I was still grinning like an idiot when he opened the door and assisted me into the car.

Between the hiking and the spa treatment, I was rather worn out, and decided to turn in early. I changed into pajamas and crawled into bed. Milo, meanwhile, took a shower.

He came out of the en suite in just a pair of sleep pants, busily drying his curls with a towel. I arched a brow over the top of my book.

"Are you *trying* to tempt me?" I inquired.

Milo gave me a quizzical look, then glanced at

his state of dress. "Oh. Uh. Not really?"

I snorted.

He sat on the end of the bed and turned on the television to check the evening news. Their main story was about a household tax vote earlier in the year and the continued unhappy response to its results, including demands for a recount. There was nothing on Ciara or Jennifer's murders.

Milo pressed the "off" button and tossed the remote on the table, before joining me under the covers. "We're outta here Monday, solved or not. What do we do if we don't find Brendan's accomplice?"

I sighed, put my bookmark back in to mark my place, and set it on the nightstand. "I don't know. I feel like I'm failing them both. Hopefully, Brendan's occupied with recovering from the nice gash I gave him, but . . . I have this horrible pit in my stomach."

"I know, *cailín*. I know." He tugged me close and pressed his face into my hair.

Somehow, I managed to put my guilt and dread aside, and went to sleep.

CHAPTER TWENTY-THREE

I was up at dawn for some reason, a somewhat horrible hour to be awake. Not even Milo, who was more of a morning person than me, was up when I found myself alert and staring at the ceiling. After about twenty minutes of trying to will myself back into unconsciousness, I got up and took a shower before getting dressed.

The sun was out, and there were small birds hopping along the edge of the little patio outside our room, looking for food. I opened the door and stepped out. The birds eyed me cautiously, then apparently decided I wasn't a threat. I took a seat on one of the white wrought-iron chairs and let the early morning sun shine down on me.

A sound nearby made me open my eyes. One

of the birds, probably some sort of finch, had moved to the table, just out of my reach. It sat there, watching me with beady little eyes.

"Good morning, birdie," I said. "If you're looking for food, I don't have any. Milo and I will probably order room service, though, after he wakes up. I'll share then."

It tipped its head and blinked rapidly. It was sort of yellow, with a pale underbelly and little pink legs. The bird cheeped at me.

"You're a brave little thing," I commented. "I saw a fox the other day and it hissed at me and ran away."

The bird just blinked again.

Reminded of my mad dash through Sligo, I looked down at my wrist. The scab was thick, the edges of the burn still an angry pink, but not the kind of an active infection. Whatever Brigit had given me had worked. My skin pulled uncomfortably when I flexed my wrist, but it didn't scream with pain as it had before.

"Made a friend, have ya?"

I jumped, and the bird fluttered off the table and to the other side of the patio, chewing Milo out thoroughly. "You scared the finch!"

"It's a warbler, not a finch," he informed me as he sat down in the other chair. His green eyes narrowed as he squinted at the bird. "Willow warbler, I'd guess."

"I told it we'd feed it and its little friend," I said, then felt stupid.

He smiled. "What do they eat?"

"Like I know? I thought it was a finch. Finches

will eat just about anything."

He turned his attention to the bird. "Y'know . . . . These warblers are usually found around bogs an' marshes, not in gardens like this one. Wonder what they're doin' here?"

A chill ran up my spine. "Bogs?" I repeated. I pressed my palm over the scab on my arm.

Milo turned sharply to look at me. "What?"

"Do you . . . Okay, this might sound completely stupid, but is it possible that it's . . . a spy or something?"

"For Brendan?" Milo frowned and shook his head. "Nah. No way. He's a creature o' darkness, y'know? Natural world hates the Fomori, far as I'm aware."

He leaned down and stretched out his hand to the warbler, whistling softly. "C'mere, wee one."

To my amazement, the warbler cocked its head, make a little "hoo-it!" sound, and hopped over to his hand. It inspected his fingers before bouncing into his grasp.

Milo picked up the bird and ran a finger over its tawny head. "You ken what I am, don'tcha?" he asked it in a whisper.

It rubbed its beak on his finger and fluttered its wings, one dark eye fixed on me.

"Close yer mouth b'fore ya catch flies," my boyfriend said mildly.

"You just- You- The-"

He rolled his eyes. "I'm a Druid an' one o' the fey, Peyton."

"I've never seen you do that before."

"Yeah, ya have. Why do ya think Angelus

likes me so much, aye?"

I blinked as rapidly as the bird. "Uh."

He set the bird on the table. "Here, keep her company while I get us some breakfast, wee one."

Milo stood up and went back into the bedroom. I stared at the bird. It stared at me.

"Do you understand us?" I asked it.

It hopped off the table and started cleaning its wing, completely dismissing me.

"You're pulling my leg with the talking to animals thing, aren't you?" I asked Milo when he came back out.

He laughed. "Little bit o' truth, *cailín*, a little bit o' blarney. Food's on its way up."

The service here was excellent and swift, which made sense, considering how expensive it was. He'd ordered French toast, sausage, and fried potatoes for both of us, and I dug in with relish. Milo had also ordered some normal toast, unbuttered, and he broke it into crumbs and scattered it for our little visitors.

I was lost in thought for most of breakfast. It wasn't 'til I was nearly done that I said, "It bothers me that I bumped into the guy, Brendan's accomplice, but for the life of me, I can't remember what he looked like. I know he was male, but that's it. I try to pull up the memory, and . . . I can see the apron from the florist, and the ballcap, but I can't see his face."

"Glamor, maybe?" Milo suggested. "Y'said Brendan looked different to ya in the cairn."

"Maybe." I poked at my food with my fork, then dropped it and swore.

Milo arched a brow, surprised by the word I'd used. "What?"

"When I described Brendan, and had Muriel draw him, I did it going off the way *I* see him. But what if all of *you* see him as the face I saw before he . . . He touched me, at the reception, and later, he said he'd 'unlocked' my abilities. I don't know what he meant, but I think I can see through his glamor. But what if you guys can't?"

Milo went pale, and repeated the word I'd used earlier. He jumped up to fetch his cell from the room. Stepping back out, he called his sister. I sat in tense silence as we waited for the phone to pick up.

It rang and rang, and apparently went to voicemail, because he hung up and shoved back his chair. "Grab yer stuff. We're goin' back. Now."

"Wait," I said, as I got up. I picked up my last sausage and shoved it in my mouth. I chewed fast, then said, "Call your dad. Have him check on her and Quinn while we're driving."

"But she hates him," he pointed out.

"I know, but he's closer to her than we are by two hundred miles, and as much as I like your sister, right now her personal safety is more important to me than her feelings."

He grimaced and handed me his phone. "You do it."

I held the phone gingerly. I hate making phone calls. I *do* it, but I hate it. And the thought of calling Lugh was terrifying.

Shoving the phone into my pocket, I hurried back in to shove my small scattering of belongings back into my bag. Feet shoved into shoes sans socks,

I grabbed my purse and was ready to go. We crammed ourselves back into the tiny two-seater car and I'd barely buckled my seatbelt when Milo floored it.

His father was already on speed-dial, probably from when they'd hunted the city looking for me. I took a deep breath before pressing the little button to make the call.

I glanced over at Milo as the phone rang. He gripped the steering wheel so tightly that his knuckles were white. With my free hand, I reached out to touch his arm.

The call went to voicemail, but before I could leave one, the phone rang. Lugh was calling me back.

"Hello?"

". . . This isn't my son. Peyton?"

"Yeah, Milo's driving at the moment. Listen, we're leaving Cork, headed back to Dublin, but . . ." I explained my worry over Brendan. "-And Muriel isn't picking up. Milo tried her cell, the house, and the shop. Quinn's cell, too."

"I'm in a meeting, but it's nothing I can't put off," he said. "I'll go check on them."

I sighed a little with relief. "Thank you so much. We'll be there as soon as we can. If . . . you find them, keep them somewhere and call me back?"

"You can be certain of that," he said, and disconnected.

I put the phone in the little cupholder on my door. "He's going to look for them."

"Good." But Milo's tension didn't ease.

***

The ride back to Dublin was quiet. I didn't want to interrupt Milo's concentration, and he wasn't in a talking mood.

We were barely out of Cork when Lugh texted that Muriel and her husband were fine, and he'd meet us at the house. When we arrived, we found his car out front. In the living room, the three of them sat in awkward silence, all of them jumping to their feet when we walked in.

"I'll be going," Lugh blurted as soon as he saw Milo. He sprang for the door and bolted from the house.

Confused, I turned to the newlyweds. "What-"

"You sent *him* to check on us?" Muriel demanded of her brother, interrupting me. "I hate him!"

"He was closer, an' there's a Fomorian after us, Muriel!" Milo snapped. "You weren't answerin' the phones. What else was I s'posed t' think? Why *didn't* you answer when I called?"

Muriel gave him an amazed look and crossed her arms. "You were outta town. Quinn an' I just got married, aye?"

I caught on a few seconds before Milo did, and I nearly had to cram my fist in my mouth to keep from laughing hysterically. When it dawned on him, my boyfriend's face went scarlet.

It took a few seconds for me to regain my composure. "Ah . . . A text of 'busy, quit bothering us' would have worked," I said diplomatically.

"Wasn't doin' much thinkin' at the time, was

I?" Muriel responded tartly, with an arch look at her twin. If anything, Milo turned even redder.

"Uh, sorry," he mumbled.

Quinn inserted himself into the conversation, looking nearly as uncomfortable. "Lugh told us your concern," he said to me. "Y' really think we can't see what he looks like?"

"I think you'd remember the solid black eyes and the ten-foot wings," I responded.

". . . Yeah, probably."

Muriel heaved a sigh, ire spent. "C'mon. If the arse has two faces, better draw t'other one."

CHAPTER TWENTY-FOUR

Muriel and I spent the next hour or so working on a sketch of Brendan's glamour face. It had more of a resemblance to Milo than I would have liked, though it was definitely the man I'd talked to at her reception.

We both shuddered, and she handed the drawing to Quinn to scan and copy. Then she retreated into her home office. After a moment, I followed.

Muriel took a seat at her worktable, picking up pliers and silver chain to continue work on the blue sapphire bracelet from before. Half her table was covered with trays and other containers, holding a variety of gems, beads, and findings.

"I do my wirework here," she told me. "Smithing's done at the shop 'cause I can make more noise there."

I poked through a small bin holding gems in individual little containers. Most were things like blue topaz, amethyst, peridot, and the like. One, however, caught my eye. It was a little bigger than a carat, cushion cut, in a deep olive green.

"What is this?" I asked Muriel.

She glanced up. "Oh, that? That's an olive tourmaline. One'a your birthstones, isn't it?"

"No idea. I know opal and rose quartz are."

She slid her chair over to a bookshelf behind her worktable, plucked a book off the shelf, and flipped through it. "Aye. Traditionally pink tourmaline, but olive also qualifies."

"Huh. That's neat."

The way the light shone through the stone, when I held it up to the light, reminded me of Milo's eyes. It was mesmerizing. Reluctantly, I put it back in the bin.

"We're plannin' on wearing our bracelets, for the funeral," Muriel said after a moment. "I wish . . . the Gardai had been able to find her things. Why would she go back out, Peyton?"

I shrugged, uncomfortable with the knowledge I carried of the things Ciara had done that night, things I wasn't about to share with Muriel. I glanced over at the ghost, currently toying with the strands of jewels that hung by the window.

Muriel looked, following my gaze. The windows were closed; the swaying of the crystals was obviously not a draft. "Ciara?" Muriel asked. "Were you wearin' the bracelet when you went back out?"

The ghost nodded. "My feet hurt, so I changed

outta the heels. Left the necklace in my flat, but I kept the bracelet on."

She looked at her empty wrist. "I'm wearin' what I did then, before he . . . took everythin' from me. But I'm not wearin' the bracelet. Why?"

Muriel raised a brow at me after I relayed this. "Why *is* that?" she asked me.

"No idea. Seriously. Nothing about this is normal for me. And it's not like I'm an expert, anyway. I operate pretty much by fumbling around blindly and waving my arms until I hit the right solution." I moved over to the window seat, under the swaying crystals, and sat down.

"Not had much experience wit' catchin' killers?" Muriel asked.

"Just one." I told her about Rob, who he'd been to me, how he'd died. I told her about my could-be friend, Lillian, who'd been mistaken for me and murdered. And I told her something I never talked about. I told her about being trapped, tied up in the kiln room of an old ceramics store, waiting with the knowledge that they were going to kill me and burn me.

She was quiet, listening. Then she got up, walked over, sat on the window seat, and leaned over to hug me tightly.

"After that," she told me, "I wouldn't be surprised if ya'd said no to helpin' Ciara. An' it nearly got ya killed this time, too. I can't tell ya how much I admire your strength, Peyton."

"Strength?" I echoed. "I'm a wuss."

She shook her head. "No. Ya *do* realize that you fought a *Fomorian* an' lived, yeah? You walked for miles, barefoot, through a peat bog an' gorse an' the rain."

I looked at the scab on my wrist. "Delirious with a fever, too."

"An' sick," she agreed. "Who else coulda done that, I ask?"

I considered that. "Buffy?"

She laughed and gave me another squeeze. "Let's make the blokes take us out on the town. How 'bout it, Buffy?"

I smiled. "Okay, that sounds good."

***

While I was dressing for our double-date, Muriel knocked on the door to my room. She carried a photo album with her, and her expression was sad.

"What's up?" I asked, opening the door to let her in.

"Just after ya headed up here, Ciara's mam called. She . . . wants some pictures for the memorial, an' . . ."

"You're having a hard time picking some?" I guessed.

Mutely, the taller woman nodded. I gestured to the bed, wordlessly taking the album out of her hands.

As we sat, I told her, "I had to do this when my mom died. It wasn't easy, and I didn't have . . . anyone to step in when I couldn't do it."

I flipped the album open as Muriel drew her legs under her. She reached out and tapped one.

"This is us at uni," she said, with a faint smile.

"Mother Mary, look at our hair!"

Darcy had tried an assymetrical bob, and it looked terrible. I had to laugh over that, but I didn't see anything odd about Muriel's hair. And Ciara's was pulled back, exposing huge, dangling earrings.

The album was arranged chronologically, and I helped Muriel select a broad example of pictures of Ciara with her dearest friends. It struck me again how I didn't have anything like this, no album full of friends and memories. Not only did I hate pictures of myself, I had pretty much one friend: Maegan. I'd had another friend, casually, named Lillian, but she'd been murdered the previous autumn, in a case of mistaken identity. Her killer had been trying for me.

If I died, who would search for images of me? And where would they find them? Note to self: let people document me a little more.

"Oh, look, this is my engagement party," Muriel said, dragging me out of my miserable thoughts.

The two pages were full of images of partiers, most of the snapshots focused on the happy couple. In the background of several, Ciara clung to a handsome, dark-haired man in a nice suit.

"Who's that?" I asked.

Muriel peered closer. "Oh, that's James. Ciara's beastly ex. He jilted her 'bout a month ago."

"So I'm guessing he won't be at the funeral?"

"Probably not, seein' as Ciara's mam didn't know him." She shrugged.

I watched as she pulled out a group shot of herself and her bridal party. The man had looked familiar, but I couldn't place him. I'd seen him recently, but when?

***

We went to see the latest blockbuster superhero movie, and then out to eat. Hoping Milo's memory was better than mine, I borrowed the album from Muriel after we got back from dinner, and showed him the photo of Ciara's boyfriend.

"We've seen him recently, but I don't recall where," I confessed.

Milo squinted at the photograph. "You're thinkin' he might be our guy?"

"I dunno. It just bugs me that he's familiar but I can't place him."

My boyfriend chewed on his lip for a moment as he peered at the glossy image. "I think . . . Is this the manager at Ciara's work?"

I took the photo from him and looked at it again. "It could be. I didn't get a really good look at the guy when we were there, but . . ."

"Wanna go back tomorrow?" Milo suggested.

"Sure. We can do that."

***

The next day started out drama-free. Muriel went to the shop on an appointment. Milo and I dropped her off and then went on a Viking boat tour that was completely cheesy. For lack of anything else to do, Milo took me to an overpriced and underwhelming "leprechaun museum". Still, it was nice to do things that didn't involve running for my life, and didn't involve bloodshed, specifically my own.

Near lunchtime, Milo called Shaunessy's to see if they had a table free for us, which they did. He casually asked if James Wooley would be working today, and got a "He's the boss, in't'he?" in return.

Outside the restaurant, I hesitated before getting out of the car. Milo hadn't opened the door for me this time, standing nearby with his keys in hand, aware enough to know that at the present time, I needed a moment. It felt a little fateful that we'd found parking right out front. Fateful, and a little ominous. Of course, everything felt ominous these days when I didn't know who the bad guy was that was working with Brendan.

I had no idea what we were walking into. A disgruntled ex was the perfect kind of suspect, though what Wooley could have to do with Brendan, I hadn't a single clue.

Finally, I pushed open the door and got out. Milo silently took my hand and we went inside. I hadn't paid much attention the first time we'd been here, as I'd mostly hung back and let Milo do the talking while I tried to "sense" anything. This time, I took in the surroundings a lot more.

It was a nice place. It wasn't hideously expensive, the prices falling about mid-range, and the decor was dark woods, creamy taupes and wines, with golden-toned lighting. It spoke of age and masculinity, though the "established" sign said they'd only been in operation four years and most of the staff was female.

We were seated at a table near the windows, a

small one set for two. The waitress who took our drinks order just happened to be the same one who'd given Milo her number last time.

"You never called me!" she said, as she handed him his Coke. "Irish boys and their glib tongues."

It was obvious she was joking, because she smiled at me and there was no hostility there.

"I wouldn't let him," I told her with a smile back.

"Ah, well, if I'd known he was taken . . ." She grinned and pretended to smack Milo with her little notebook. "You let me think you were available!"

He looked chagrined. "Sorry."

She laughed, then said, "Oh, forgot to say, I'm Mary. Your man here knows that already, so I didn't think t'tell ya. You want an appetizer or anythin'?"

I shook my head. "No, thanks."

"I'll just leave you to look over those menus, then."

She went off with a swing of her red ponytail. I glanced up to find Milo eyeing me.

"What?"

"A week ago, ya woulda been contemplatin' killing the girl with yer fork."

"A lot's changed in a week," I pointed out. "I nearly died--again--and . . ."

"Aye."

Mary came back after a few minutes. I ordered parmesan-crusted chicken with locally-grown mashed potatoes, while Milo chose a steak.

When we were relatively alone once more, I looked around the restaurant. "I don't see Wooley anywhere."

"Might be in a back office or somethin'."

"True."

When Mary brought our food, she was a little more subdued. As she put our plates down, she said, "I'm sorry to be bringin' up somethin' sad, but do ya know when Ciara's services might be?"

There was a little lump in my stomach. I'd forgotten momentarily that she'd known Ciara, and for Mary, her friend's death was likely a baffling and terrifying mystery with no answers yet given. There was no way I was volunteering the horrors I knew.

"Friday, three," Milo put in quietly. He told her where, and she nodded.

"I'll tell the others. Thanks."

She disappeared again.

I poked my fork into the chicken breast, my appetite somewhat diminished by the reminder of our real reason for visiting. "So, random question, but I've been wondering . . ."

"What's that?" Milo's appetite seemed to have suffered nothing, as he dug into his steak with relish.

"That whole thing about not saying thank you or stuff like that, does that apply to . . . you know?"

He snorted, nearly inhaling a bite of beef. "Hell, no. Da says that's bollocks. I asked him meself, t'other day, when we were drivin' 'round lookin' for ya. Gives you lots of time t' talk, stuck in a car drivin' cross the bloody country."

I sipped my soda, decided to take a bite of the chicken. It was delicious, and it helped make me hungry again. "Iron allergy, or any metals?"

"Nope."

"Inability to cross running water?"

He laughed. "No, not true."

"Okay, what folklore *is* true?"

"Time passes differently 'tween here an' Tir na n'Og." A shadow flickered over his face. "'Course, we knew that one. Leprechauns aren't real, but ya still don't wanna trust most of Da's people. Not that they come 'round here much. Da says it's him, the triplets, Brigit, couple others, is all. Manannán. But only 'cause he has t' hang around, t' pick up souls."

"But most are dead or . . . keep to themselves?"

He nodded. "Da said ten at most are still in the modern world."

"Ten more than I knew existed a year ago. Heck, even six months ago."

"Same here," he said dryly.

Mary came back to refill our drinks, and Milo asked if her boss was around.

For a moment, she looked confused as to why we'd want to speak with her boss, then she said, "Oh, right. That. Guess Muriel toldja 'bout him an' Cee. Despicable, I thought it was, but durin' a separation, I guess anythin' goes."

"Separation?" I echoed.

"Oh, aye. Jim an' Ciara were all hot while he an' his wife were separated, but they reconciled an' one o' Peggy's conditions was he stop seein' Ciara." She clapped a hand over her mouth. "I shouldna said any o' that."

"Don't worry," I assured her. "It won't go any further than us."

She mumbled something and scurried off.

"Well," Milo said slowly, drawing the word out to several syllables. "That's somethin' interesting t'learn."

"I'll say." I drank half my soda in one go. "You think his . . . way to ditch the girlfriend to please the wife was to turn her over to Brendan?"

"Maybe."

We ate our food, and we waited, but Wooley didn't make an appearance. Mary had confirmed he was here, but he apparently didn't want to talk to us. Guilt, or something else?

Finally, we decided to call it, and asked for the check. As we left, I said, "It's not like we can confront him and demand to know if he killed her."

"He didn't," Milo pointed out. "Brendan did. At most, he's an accessory."

"True." I sighed. "I wonder if he'll show up to the funeral?"

My boyfriend shrugged. This time, he opened the door for me and I climbed into the car. I stared at the restaurant. Movement at one of the windows caught my eye. Wooley's face appeared for a moment. He saw me looking, and yanked the drapes closed.

"Huh."

"What?"

"Mr. Avoidant just saw us. He didn't look happy."

Milo started the car. "Well, he can stay that way. Let's go back to th'shop."

CHAPTER TWENTY-FIVE

Muriel was more than happy to let us hang out with her for the afternoon. Milo entertained himself while I got a lesson in jewelry-making from his sister.

Shortly after four, the front door banged open and James Wooley stormed in, decked out in a fancy three-piece suit. I was so startled, I dropped the pliers I'd been using to awkwardly make a wire-wrapped beaded chain.

"The hell do you think you're doing, coming to my place of business to harass me?" he demanded. I'd assumed he was Irish, but he was, surprisingly, as American as me. And I was apparently his target, because he tried to come past the counter into the workroom beyond.

Milo inserted himself in Wooley's way. The shorter man stopped, realizing how much Milo towered over him. "We're not harassin' anyone, Mr. Wooley. Muriel recommended the restaurant, an' we went to try it. We also went to extend funeral invitations to Ciara's friends."

Unable to resist a smart remark, I added, "Besides, harassment requires interaction of some sort, and you wouldn't come talk to us."

"Peyton," Muriel cautioned.

"What? It's the truth. Dining at his restaurant and asking the waitress if he was at work, and asking to speak with him? That's not harassment." I narrowed my eyes at Wooley. "You're on the offensive, which means we hit a nerve. All we did was ask to talk to you. We didn't even say what about."

Wooley scoffed and crossed his arms, defensive posturing at its finest now as he leaned back a little from Milo. "Obviously, you wanted to talk to me about Ciara."

"Well, yeah. We wanted to invite you to her funeral. But since you're married, I'd imagine I'd imagine your wife would frown on that." I moved so Milo wasn't blocking me. Wooley's attention stayed on me, which was interesting. Maybe it was because we were both American.

"No, she wouldn't," he said shortly. "And why do you care, anyway, if I'm offensive or defensive or whatever?"

I rolled my shoulders. "Just seems you're on the attack, which indicates you have something to hide."

"Hide?" he repeated incredulously. "What would I hide?"

Wooley stared for a moment, then horror washed over him. "You don't . . . you don't think I killed Ciara, do you? God. I could never hurt her. I loved her."

"But you loved your wife more?" Milo asked softly.

"Well, yeah. My wife and I have two children together." His anger suddenly deflated. "And the Gardai already questioned me. I have alibis for the night she went missing, and the night she was found. Thursday, I was at the restaurant 'til close. Then I spent the rest of the night at home with my wife. On Saturday, we were in Belfast with my wife's parents, for my daughter's birthday. Happy?"

Not really, since it had blown my theory to pieces, but I nodded.

He glared at both of us, and said, "You're banned from Shaunessy's. You show up, I'll call the cops."

We watched in silence as he left. I looked up at Milo.

Behind us, Muriel said, "Well, that was entertainin'. This what you always do?"

Wryly, as I stooped to retrieve the pliers, I said, "Unfortunately, that happens a lot in my line of work."

***

For the funeral on Friday afternoon, I pulled out the little black dress I'd originally brought to wear to Muriel's wedding, before I'd been roped into this whole fiasco. It was sleeveless, so I borrowed a pretty, black crocheted shawl that Muriel had in the shop, one Eithne had made.

My plaid flats seemed a little festive for the occasion, but it was those, my brown leather walking shoes I usually wore to work--not very pretty--or my garish pink slippers. I slipped on the blue and grey shoes. Digging in my toiletries bag for my makeup, I spotted the bracelet Muriel had given me, and remembered that she'd said "we" were all wearing them in honor of Ciara. I fastened the chain around my wrist, slapped on a muted lipstick, and combed my fingers through my stick-straight hair. I'd considered curling it or something, and had opted not to. I fastened the matrix opal necklace Muriel had also made around my neck, and with it hanging at the hollow of my throat, and the gold medallion from Lugh nestled between my breasts, I felt as prepared as I was likely to get.

As I came out of my room, Muriel took a look at the bandage on my wrist and motioned for me to follow her. The infection was gone, leaving just the scab and healing skin, so other than putting a wide bandage on it to cover, I wasn't thinking much about it anymore.

Muriel handed me a hinged cuff bracelet, just wide enough to cover the supposedly skin-colored material. "Here. Just so ya don't get odd questions."

Slipping it on reminded me of Brigit when she'd shown me her own scar, and a chill ran down my spine. The bracelet was pretty, though, silver with an etched floral design. It wasn't one of Muriel's pieces; I could tell by the feel that it was only silver-toned, likely brass or copper underneath. If I wore it too long, it would lose the finish. I'd have to take it off after the funeral.

I don't like funerals. I only attended my mother's because, well, she was my mother. And she would have made my life very difficult if I hadn't. She'd spent the whole time making snide remarks about the speakers. Her humor, in relief that she was no longer in pain, had been one of the only things that got me through it.

There was no such saving grace here. I sat in silence beside Milo, too painfully aware of Darcy in the row behind us, glaring a hole in the back of my head. Ciara's mother, Deirdre Murphy, sobbed through most of the proceedings. James Wooley had not made an appearance, not that I'd truly expected him to.

Halfway through the service, I felt my bracelet slip from my wrist. It landed in my lap, nearly sliding to the floor, but I managed to snag it at the last second. The clasp had caught on something and was a little bent, just enough for the spring mechanism to malfunction. I made a mental note to show it to Muriel, and slipped it into the small, zippered compartment inside my purse.

Milo and Quinn had offered to be pallbearers, and they helped carry Ciara's simple, elegant coffin to and from the hearse. It brought back too many memories of my mother's burial, and once again I found myself missing her terribly. True, she might have been hanging around as a ghost, but it wasn't the same. It was all the more painful for Ciara's mother's wailing.

Contrary to the usual weather, it was sunny out, as if Mother Nature were being perverse. After they lowered the coffin into the ground, I took a moment to wander around amongst the headstones. It was a really, really big cemetery. Milo followed me in silence, much as we'd done at Glendalough. There were ghosts here, too, but none paid us any attention.

Milo showed me some famous residents, and told me stories of those I didn't recognize. Eventually, we headed back to where his sister and her husband waited, having expressed their condolences.

"I want to find this guy," I said fiercely, as we drove away. "No mother should have to go through this for their child. Not this way."

My boyfriend gripped my hand and gave it a squeeze, but didn't speak.

***

There was a gathering at the Murphy home after, which Muriel and Quinn went to. I didn't feel at all comfortable going, so Milo and I declined to join them. Since we still had the rental, he and I headed into the city proper. Ciara had stayed behind with her mother, even though the woman couldn't see her.

"Your mother makes really pretty things," I said, fingering the edge of the shawl that I still wore. "I'm a bit sad to give this back."

"Keep it," he said. "I'll buy it off Mure b'fore

we leave. An' make Da pay for it."

I smiled briefly, but mirth felt wrong. "Well, I guess Lugh *does* owe her a crapload of back child support."

Milo snorted softly. "Aye, that's the least he owes her."

"How do you feel about taking his money?" I asked.

He shrugged his shoulder, just the one, as he made a left onto Dame Street. "Part o' me hates it. Part o' me . . . thinks it's nice t'not struggle anymore. He says he'll give me anythin' I want, as much money as I want. I don't . . . wanna become dependent on it, y'know?"

I nodded. "What if he vanishes again?"

"'Zactly."

We parked in the garage nearest Muriel's shop. I changed out of my black flats and into the more comfortable pink slippers, and we wandered by the store to check on things. Milo found the locks still secure, windows all intact, and texted his sister that all was well there. I left the bracelet I'd borrowed from Muriel in her desk in the workroom.

As we stepped back out, I noticed the day had grown a little chilly, and I pulled the shawl closer. Waiting as Milo locked the doors again, I looked around idly.

Standing across the street, watching us with a scowl on his face, was Brendan. His black eyes narrowed with hatred, wings of shadow seeming to create an alcove to hide in against the wall of the building opposite. Just a mere twenty feet away.

I gasped and stepped back, bumping into Milo.

My heart pounded in my ears, my hands going cold and clammy.

A green Dublin Bus went by.

When it passed, Brendan was gone.

Milo's hands curved over my shoulders. "Y'alright?" he inquired. "What happened?"

"Brendan," I choked out. "I saw Brendan. He was here."

CHAPTER TWENTY-SIX

Naturally, Milo looked around with alarm, but Brendan was nowhere to be seen.

We spent the next two and a half hours looking for the Fomorian, though I honestly wasn't sure what Milo thought we were going to do if we found him. We were both seriously outmatched, had no weapons, and no clue how to deal with him. I didn't, however, point that out to Milo as I tagged along behind him, my hand in his.

Eventually, he admitted defeat. My stomach was growling by then, and he conceded that we needed to eat, since lunch had been hours ago.

Whiskey Fish was close by, and I suggested we go there. I wasn't sure what kept drawing me back to the place, but of all the places we'd gone that unfortunate night, that was the only one that resonated with me.

There were over six hundred pubs in Dublin, and I wasn't aware of any that only served alcohol. This was no exception, offering a fairly substantial menu. We had to order at the bar. Declan was tending again, and he smiled as he greeted us.

"Can't stay away, huh?" he asked. "What can I getcha?"

Milo ordered a beer; I opted for a Coke. I was craving a Dr Pepper, but they apparently didn't have that in Ireland. First thing I did when I got home was going to be buying a huge bottle of it.

I glanced over the menu, the offerings printed on somewhat plain cardstock and laminated, the placard scarred and bent on all the corners. As I perused, Milo told Declan, "We just came from a funeral."

"Ahh, aye, that girl you were in askin' about last week, was it?" The bartender nodded. "Sad business, that. Speakin' of, the bouncer ya talked to up an' quit on me. The Gardai were in lookin' for him, an' he took off after that."

Declan handed Milo his Guinness. My boyfriend thanked him, said, "Huh. Did seem the flighty type. Garda say anythin' to ya 'bout him?"

"Not word one," Declan said. "Gotta wonder, though, with him just skivvin' off like that, he didn't have somethin' t'do with that poor girl."

I accepted my Coke, murmured something non-committal, and sipped from the glass.

"So what'll ya have?" Declan asked me.

"Mm. I think I'll go with the stew and bread," I told him.

"Same for me," Milo put in.

Declan called the order to the cook. "So what've you heard?" he asked Milo. "Anythin' from the Gardai on yer end?"

"Not a thing." Milo lied smoothly, sipping from his own glass. "Me sister's real broke up about it. I'm guessin' it's one'a those things never gets solved, like that . . . who was it, *cailín*, that actress back inna '40s?"

I had to think for a minute. "The Black Dahlia? Elizabeth Short, I think. Yeah, they never solved that one."

Declan leaned forward on the bar, the neck of his polo gaping a little to hint at a tattoo just left of his neck, on his collarbone. "Aye? And who's 'at? Never heard of her."

"Oh, she was an actress, mostly did bit parts, I think. Most famous thing about her is that she was found in an empty lot in the Los Angeles area, cut in half."

Something flickered across his face, possibly disgust. It was hard to tell in the somewhat dim interior. "That's shameful. An' they never found who did it?"

"Nope. Crime scene was a complete mess, there were reporters acting like cops and hiding information, and they wasted a bunch of time chasing a guy who wasn't connected to it." Tired of holding the cold glass, I put it down and drummed my fingers on the bar. "My mom was fascinated by it. She was kind of a horror freak."

Milo tipped his head in curiosity. "Really?"

"Oh, yeah. Why do you think she wrote books about medieval castles and all the people murdered there?"

"Hadn't thought about it."

A tall, thin woman, a little younger than me by the looks of her, came into the pub. She tottered on high heels, her slender legs encased in skinny jeans. Her top half was covered in a tank top and a too-large dolman sweater that hung off one shoulder. She had horrifically teased brown hair and big, gold hoop earrings. My first thought was "hooker".

"Dec!" she caroled. "Can I bum the car off ya for a bit, lovey?"

"Yeah, sure," he said distractedly. "Keys are me jumper over there."

She tip-toed over to the aforementioned cardigan, hanging on a hook behind the bar. I watched with vague amusement as she reached into the pocket and fished for the keys. Seriously, how hard was it? Judging from the way she stuck her tongue out and went cross-eyed, very. In the struggle, she managed to knock a herribone tweed flatcap from where it'd hung above the cardigan.

Milo leaned over and kissed my temple, asking under his breath, "Inbreeding?"

It took everything I had not to burst out laughing. The urge only got worse when she wailed, "Dec, the keys're stuck!"

Declan rolled his eyes. "'Scuse me," he said to us, and took the handful of steps over to the hook. He reached up to pull the sweater down. As he did, the neck of his tee pulled even more, revealing a tattoo of a square cross.

"They're caught on something," he muttered. "Just a sec, love."

Something in the back of my brain pinged, and I tried to catch it as I watched the bartender pull the keys out. Something silver was tangled around the keys, snagged in the knit of the sweater. The bimbo cooed.

"Oh, you remembered!" she chirped, and lightning-fast, had it untangled. Funny how that skill had evaded her just moments before.

She held it up, and Declan snatched at it, trying to take it back.

"Am I ruinin' the surprise?" she laughed.

"Fallon," he said, voice dropping. "Give it back."

Hey, Bimbo had a name. Fallon danced out of his grasp, but she caught a heel in a knot in the floorboards and nearly went down. The piece of jewelry hit the floor with a muted rattle and slid towards me, stopped at my stool.

I was off the stool and bending to pick it up before I'd thought of it, and I plucked the silver bracelet off the floor. A gold heart, wrapped in silver wire, held a little emerald briolette, shiny gold beads on silver links winking in the dim light. My skin went cold as I touched it.

"Pretty," I commented, though how I got anything out was beyond me.

"I've the best lad!" Fallon told me, and batted her overdone lashes at him.

I knew the bracelet, knew it well. I had one just like it in my purse. There was only one place this could have come from, and with that realization came recognition of the cross on Declan's arm: St. Bridget's Cross.

Ciara. It was Ciara's bracelet.

Declan, suddenly at my side, grabbed the bracelet from my numb fingers. When his fingers touched mine, I caught a flash of him plucking a paper out of the trash, one with Ciara's number on it. The one Tom had thrown away.

He gave me a look I couldn't read, and shoved the bracelet at Fallon. "Yeah, yeah. Happy anniversary, love. Take the car, I'm servin' customers."

I don't know how I managed, but somehow, I picked up my soda, gave Declan a nod in thanks, and went across the pub to a table. By the time I reached it, I was shaking. Milo followed and helped me into a chair.

"What's wrong?" he asked. "Your hands're like ice!"

"The bracelet," I breathed. "Milo, I need your phone."

Frowning, he pulled it from his pocket and handed it to me. "What about the bracelet?"

"In my purse, there's a little zipper pocket," I said softly. "There's a piece of paper in it, would you get it for me?"

He looked at the purse hanging from my shoulder, but didn't ask why *I* wasn't fetching it. Milo pulled my purse over, opened it, and unzipped the pocket. Mature guy he was, he didn't react to the tampons I had stuffed in there. He retrieved the paper, and then his eyes widened when he saw my broken bracelet.

"It-" he began.

"Shhh," I whispered. "Gimme the paper."

Wordlessly, Milo handed me the scrap I'd scrawled Byrne's mobile number on. Milo had already called him before; I hadn't really needed him to get me the number, it had been an excuse to show him the bracelet without drawing attention to the fact that I had it.

I glanced over at the bar, where Declan was occupied draughting a pint. "He's got a cross tattooed on his collar bone," I murmured.

Milo started to turn, but I shook my head. "Don't look at him."

I pulled up the text messages and put in Byrne's number. Then I typed a message and sent it off.

IT'S THE (IN)CONVENIENT AMERICAN. ARE YOU IN THE CITY?

A minute ticked by, then two. Then Milo's phone vibrated.

YES. HOW DID YOU GET THIS NUMBER?

WE CALLED YOU ABOUT VAN, REMEMBER? YOU NEED TO COME TO WHISKEY FISH NOW.

Another minute passed. I smiled at the phone, as if amused by the text exchange. I was anything but.

WHY?

I sighed. BECAUSE BARTENDER HAD CIARA MURPHY'S BRACELET. THERE ARE ONLY 6 IN WORLD. MURIEL MADE. HE GAVE TO GIRL NAMED FALLON?

This time, there was a very long pause. I could almost picture Byrne trying to decide whether to trust me, or whether to turn his phone off. He was probably beating his head against something in indecision. Did I know for certain? No, but it's what I'd be doing in the situation.

WHY ARE YOU THERE?

That one made me smile for real. BECAUSE IT'S CLOSE 2 MURIEL'S SHOP? JUST WANDERED IN, I SWEAR. BAD LUCK MAGNET. R YOU COMING?

STAY THERE, KEEP EYE ON HIM. AND WHICH BARTENDER?

DECLAN. HIS GF TOOK HIS CAR, SHOULD BE BACK SOON?

DON'T TRY ANYTHING. LET ME KNOW IF HE MOVES.

OK. PLEASE HURRY.

I closed the texts and handed the phone back to

Milo. He tucked it into the inner pocket of his suit jacket.

"What was that about?" he asked. "Looked entertaining."

"Oh, just texting Adam, invited him for drinks."

Milo gave me a look. "And how *is* Adam?"

He'd caught on. Adam wasn't here, but Adam was a detective. "Oh, he's grand. Said he'd be here in a few and to save him a seat."

Translation: stay put.

Milo nodded and sipped his Guinness. "Cool."

"So, what do we have left to do on the itinerary?" I asked, in a more normal voice.

"We could go by UCD, I could show ya where I went to school. Granted, it ain't as old or distinguished as Trinity, but . . ."

"I'd like that," I said, and meant it.

A woman in black slacks and a dark green shirt with the pub's logo on it came over with two trays and set them on the table. "Name's Meggy. Give a shout if ya need anyt'in', right?"

Aaaaand, she was gone again.

"Wow," I said.

"What?"

"I think that's the first time in the entire history of our relationship that a woman hasn't paid you *any* attention when we're out at a restaurant."

He burst out laughing.

"What?" I demanded.

"Ah, *cailín*. I don't even notice 'em 'cause I got you."

I flushed and looked down at my stew.

"'m serious," he said, though he was still grinning. "I adore you."

Nonplussed still, I concentrated on my stew. It was okay, not the best I'd had--the fare at Milo's cousin's pub back in Utah was so much better--and it was difficult to really enjoy it as I waited anxiously for our police "friend".

Outside, what little sun we'd seen earlier was gone, which meant it was after eight. Where had the day gone? With the sun set, they turned on more of the overhead lights to compensate. In all honesty, it didn't help much.

Byrne didn't keep us waiting long. He strolled in about twenty minutes after I'd texted him, his reddish hair reflecting the light from the ceiling. I would have known it was him even if he hadn't scanned the room, spotted us, and nodded.

There were more people coming in by the minute. That was going to make things difficult if Declan made a run for it. I hoped he didn't.

Byrne swung by the table. "Evening," he said, trying for amiable and failing. "Tell me about this bracelet."

I used the cop for cover, pulling my broken bracelet out to show it to him. "This one's mine. All the bridesmaids and Muriel have one. We wore them today for Ciara's funeral, so I know it isn't anyone else's. Declan wasn't at the funeral, so . . ."

Byrne's mouth pressed into a hard line. "Yes, I see your point."

"He mentioned that you came in to talk to Tom, and that Tom's missing?"

The detective inspector nodded. "Completely

vanished. Honestly, we were suspectin' him 'til I got your message."

"What're you gonna do?" Milo inquired.

"Talk to him. Stay here."

We watched, food forgotten, as he pushed his way through the patrons to the bar. Declan greeted him, then realized who he was talking to. Even from over here, his fidgeting was apparent. Cut out for a life of crime, this man was not.

It was impossible to tell what the two were saying, but Declan shook his head. He feigned shock--again, obvious--and pushed back from the bar.

Fallon walked back in, waving Declan's keys. Over the general din, I heard her say, "I'm back, lovey, you miss me?"

The bracelet taken from Ciara glittered on her wrist. Declan looked at it, looked at Byrne.

Then he vaulted over the bar, knocking down two customers, and ran for the door.

Byrne shoved after him, shouting for him to stop. Milo sprang up. He wasn't closer to the door, but he was a lot faster than the detective.

More out of not wanting to be left behind than any need to chase the guy, I got up and followed. Declan got to the door, slammed into it, and was gone into the night.

There was no way I could keep up; all of the men had longer legs than me, and my feet were still on the raw side. I was also short of breath and had to stop to gasp in air. But I tried anyway. I must have made quite the sight, running in my fuzzy slippers down Merrion Row, after several men. Fortunately, there weren't that many people out and about in this section of town.

I reached the corner of Kildare Street just as Milo caught up with Declan and grabbed him by the arm. Byrne was still ten feet back. Two Garda who'd joined us in the chase blew past me, but all they had were stun-guns, and they weren't good at a distance, or for threatening anyone into submission.

Declan had more experience with brawling than Milo, and even as my boyfriend hauled him around, the bartender ducked and slammed his free fist into Milo's stomach. It doubled him over with a "whoof!" I could hear from half a block away.

Taking advantage of Milo's slackened grip, Declan tore free and took off running.

"Halt!" one of the guards shouted.

Declan glanced back, over his shoulder, as he stepped off the curb. Ciara suddenly appeared behind him, put her hands on his shoulders, and *shoved* him--

--right into the path of the Dublin Ghost Bus as it trundled around the corner and onto St Stephen's Green.

The bus slammed on its brakes and its tires squealed. I slapped my hands over my eyes, but couldn't block out the thud and the crunch as Declan collided with the front end of the bus and fell under the wheels.

Hands caught my shoulders, gently, and Milo turned me away from the scene. "Don't look," he advised. "It's bad."

"Wasn't planning on it," I said in a weak, tight voice. Nausea threatened and I pressed a hand hard to my mouth.

"Guess that wrecks all fond memories we'll have of the tour," Milo mused.

I choked out a miserable laugh. "Oh, geez. Those poor tourists. They got so much more than they paid for."

"Windows are curtained," he pointed out. "Hopefully, they didn't see a thing."

One of the guards called to us, and I turned, as Milo did, when the uniformed officer approached. I caught a glimpse, out of the corner of my eye, of a tattooed arm sticking out from under one of the tires, and my stomach revolted.

I barely made it to the nearest trash can before I lost it.

Milo led me across the street to the park and sat me on a bench to wait for the Gardai, away from the grisly accident site. I shivered and he shed his jacket, draping it over my shoulders.

"That was awful," I whispered. "I'm never gonna get that sound out of my head."

He kissed my temple and hugged me close. "S'okay, *cailín*. I think it's over now."

"Brendan's still out there, somewhere," I reminded him.

"Problem for another day," he told me softly.

Ciara popped into view right in front of me, and I jumped. After a moment, I realized she looked different. It took several seconds of hard staring to put my finger on it.

"You have eyes," I said stupidly.

"I feel a hell of a lot better, too," she said cheerfully. "Still dead, but then, so's that bastard."

"So it was definitely him."

She nodded. "Remembered soon as you touched my bracelet. All came back to me."

"That's . . . good."

"I'm not goin' for good just yet, but I'll get outta yer hair."

And she vanished.

Byrne appeared on the path and wearily came to join us, though he remained standing. "Well, that's one very flat barkeep," he said after a moment. "Some of my men found the girl, got the bracelet from her."

He held up the evidence bag, then stuffed it in his pocket. "He doesn't live too far from here, so we'll be goin' by his place. Wonder if he's got anything else of Miss Murphy's. I'd say this was a damned shame, him escapin' justice, but I don't think our system could give him a more fitting punishment than execution by double decker, after what he did to that girl."

Det. Ins. Byrne took a good look at me. "You alright, there, Miss Reynolds?"

"I just saw a guy get squished by a bus," I said.

"Point taken. Go home, you two. I'll be by in the mornin' to take formal statements."

Milo kissed the top of my head, then helped me to my feet. "C'mon. Let's go."

We took the path through the park, rather than go out the entrance closest to the scene, and made our way back to the car. On our walk, Milo called his father.

"Dunno if you heard," he said, "but the guy who kidnapped Ciara an' the florist just got himself run over on St Stephen's."

Lugh said something, and Milo said, "Right. Be there soon."

He put the phone away, telling me, "Detour. Lugh's requested we give *him* a statement."

At least with Lugh, we could be completely honest about the evening's events.

CHAPTER TWENTY-SEVEN

Brigit and two of the triplets were at Lugh's place when Milo and I arrived. The one I thought was Bonnie took one look at me and dragged me over to the sofa to sit down.

"Lugh says ya found the man an' he got smushed by a bus," she said. "Musta been awful."

"He went crunch," I said weakly. "And I threw up."

She tsked. "Erin, *deirfiúr*, go down t' that place wi' the big M on it, two blocks down, wouldja?"

"It's called McDonald's," her sister informed her.

"Aye, that one. Get Peyton somethin' to eat. What do ya like?" Bonnie asked me.

"Um." I shook my head. "Not really hungry, but I love French fries."

Erin peered at me and said, "Maybe some meat in ya, too. You're awful pale."

I wasn't about to argue. Erin took off, and Brigit came to sit beside me on the sofa. She handed me a mug of hot tea.

"This'll settle you," she told me.

"Thanks," I said gratefully, more for the warmth of the mug than anything else. My hands had been so cold since I'd touched that bracelet.

"So what happened?" Lugh asked.

Milo gave him the run-down, with occasional interjections from me. I explained that I'd seen Brendan outside Muriel's shop, and told them about the vision I'd had at the pub.

"-and then Ciara appeared outta nowhere, an' pushed him under the bus," Milo concluded.

We all took a moment ponder that.

Milo's cell rang. He answered it, and mouthed, "Muriel."

"Do you think Brendan followed you, or was he watching the shop?" Lugh asked me.

I pulled the necklace from my dress. "I'm still wearing this, so he's gotta be watching the shop."

He frowned fiercely. "I don't want to tell Muriel to close it or move it, but if he knows where it is . . ."

"We could rent out the space beside it," Brigit suggested. "Keep a guard or two there under some front."

Lugh nodded. "Excellent idea."

"I do occasionally have them, yes," she

snarked. "Do the police need you for anything more tonight?"

I shook my head. "Nope. Detective Inspector Byrne said he's going to stop by Muriel's tomorrow to get our statements. But . . . Brendan aside, I think it's over."

Milo came back in the room. "Muriel wanted t'know why we weren't back yet. I told her what happened. She had a fit, o' course."

"Of course."

"I'll follow the two of you back," Lugh said. "Just in case."

"I'm not leaving before I get my fries," I put in.

Failinis padded in. He perked up when he saw me and hurried over, shoving his big face into my lap. I had to use both hands to pet his massive head.

"Hi, doggy!" I said. "How's the big puppy, huh?"

He wagged his tail and drooled on my skirt.

"I'll pay for dry cleaning," Lugh said.

"Eh, it's wash and wear," I told him.

The dog nuzzled his head against my stomach and sighed happily. I wondered vaguely if he had some healing properties, because I felt steadier the more I pet him.

Erin came back with two burgers and two buckets of fries, giving half of her haul to Milo. I inhaled mine, surprisingly hungry. I'd had no appetite until I'd smelled the fries.

Failinis tried to con some fries out of me. I snuck him one when Lugh wasn't looking.

***

When we got up to leave, I offered my borrowed credit card back to Lugh, but he held up a hand.

"Keep it," he said. "You, too, Milo. You may need it in days t'come, and Goddess knows I owe you both so much."

Hesitantly, I put it back in my purse.

"Get an international plan," the *Tuatha* king said then. "Use the card to pay for it. Ring me if you have questions about your calling."

"Okay."

He handed me a business card, to make sure I had his information. I looked it over. It said, "Liam MacKeen, CEO" and listed *Caomhnú Éire* as a "private conservation firm" with an address on Merrion Street. I realized it was this building.

"Do you . . . own the building?" I asked.

He nodded. "We have to, for security."

"Oh."

Brigit walked us to the door. "If you need anything," she told me, "call Lugh. I'll come."

"You're like my own, private Galadriel," I joked.

She smirked. "Where do you think Tolkien got his inspiration for her?" she asked, and shut the door.

Toasted

Chapter Twenty-Eight

We returned to Muriel's. I, for one, slept like the dead. We didn't have much to say when Byrne came in the morning for our statements. I couldn't tell him anything Ciara had told me, and since the guy was dead, it was pretty much just a formality.

They'd searched Declan's flat and found more of Ciara's things, and a few things stolen from the florist's shop. As far as the police were concerned, he'd been a psycho who liked to mutilate girls. What they couldn't explain was why he'd gone to Muriel's wedding. We didn't really have any answers for them, or for ourselves. I couldn't remember the face of the man who'd delivered the flowers. For all I knew, Brendan had done that.

When I asked about Tom, who'd disappeared,

Byrne told me he'd apparently been skimming from the till and had skipped the country when the police started sniffing around. At least, that was the assumption. They couldn't find him, and bank records showed more deposits than his wages and tips could account for. The day before he'd disappeared, he'd withdrawn everything and bought a plane ticket to Germany. I was a little relieved that he didn't seem to be one of Brendan or Declan's victims, despite his being a skeeze.

As for what to do about the Fomorian, it wasn't in my hands. As High King, that was Lugh's job, and I was more than happy to let him take over.

Our last few days in Ireland were spent doing nothing, which was fine with me. I'd had enough adventure and excitement to last me a good, long time. I had good memories of Ireland, but I also had some really nasty ones that I wanted desperately to leave behind me.

And I missed my cat, and my best friend, and my ghost of a mother.

Muriel and Quinn saw us off at the airport. As we exchanged hugs and good-byes, I noticed Muriel slip something to her brother and wink. It wasn't my business, however, so I didn't ask. Milo stuffed whatever it was into the pocket of his jeans, and hugged her.

"Well," Quinn said to me. "It was lovely meeting you, strange as this visit's been."

"Same to you! I'm sorry your honeymoon got ruined."

He shrugged. "I have my girl, I'm happy enough with that."

I impulsively embraced him, quickly, then turned to hug Muriel.

"You take care," she told me. "Don't be gettin' yerself kidnapped again."

"I will do my utmost best," I replied solemnly. "You do the same."

She sighed. "Aye, well. I know what he looks like now, so I can watch out for him."

I wished her good luck, and then Milo and I had to go take our place in the line through airport security.

"You ready t'go home?" Milo asked me.

"Definitely."

"Good. Let's go home."

For those readers not familiar with Celtic mythology, I've included a quick guide to the individuals appearing in this book, or those mentioned frequently.

Balor - King of the Fomorians, slain by his grandson, Lugh.

Banba, Eriu, and **Fohla** - triplets, also called a triple goddess, these three are the goddesses for whom Ireland was named. Also fertility goddesses. Married three brothers, who were responsible in legend for the death of Lugh. Nieces by marriage to Brigit.

Brigit - Daughter of Daghda (son of Danu and Bile), wife of Tuireann. Had three sons, who were responsible for killing Cian, father of Lugh. Goddess of Fertility.

Danu - The Mother goddess, who created the world and lent her name to the *Tuatha Dé Danann* (People of the Goddess Danu).

Lugh Lambfadha - Son of Cian (son of Dian Cecht) and Ethlinn (daughter of Balor). God of light. Slew the king of the Fomorians, Balor, and succeeded Nuada to the throne of the *Tuatha Dé Danann.*

Manannán - Foster father of Lugh, also the

sea god of Celtic mythology and responsible for escorting souls to the other side.

M. Roberg

Toasted

Marianna Roberg has been a costume designer, a website designer, a slush pile reader for a science fiction and fantasy magazine, and con committee for *Life, the Universe, and Everything,* Brigham Young University's symposium on sci-fi and fantasy.

She lives in Utah with her family and two cats, and makes jewelry in her spare time. Readers can visit her website at www.mdroberg.net.